HELGA

Marie London

ISBN:9798794983579

Introduction

It was November 1940 in Roskilde, a small town, a few miles outside Copenhagen.

Denmark had declared itself neutral at the start of WW2 but Germany had only taken six hours to occupy the country. Times were hard but even harder if you had a father like Ralph.

The girls huddled together in the corner of the kitchen. Their father was in one of his drunken rages again and their mother was receiving the full force of his fist.

Helga and Anna had witnessed their mother being beaten many many times and they were absolutely petrified. Ralph was a womaniser and a drunk .Greta was his punching bag. The girls had learnt to do as they were told and keep out of their fathers way as much as possible to avoid contact with his fist. Unfortunately that was not always possible.

Chapter One

Helga could hear her dog barking in the distance as she laid in her bed looking up at the ceiling making pictures with the shadows. She thought of her sister Anna and hoped she was happy now she had escaped from her awful life here in the place she should have felt safe. Helga was missing Anna but she was glad she had embraced the opportunity to marry Peter and start her married life in Copenhagen.She knew her sister was lucky to have met a good man who had taken her away from her unhappy life here in Roskilde and the beatings she had received from their father.She was also sad she couldn't have gone to live with her. Anna was 17 and Helga was only 13, too young to leave home.

Helga was thankful it was the weekend because she didn't have to go to school and get taunted by the other children. The children in her class didn't like her and used to kick her as she walked past them. One girl used to spit at her and called her horrible names. Her mind wandered to last summer when she was happy going on picnics with Anna and Peter. She had become friends with Walter who was Peters young brother. She always had fun with those people and her sister was the best friend anyone could ever have. Now things had changed. When Anna had left the town to live in the city Walter had gone with them as he had no other family. The three important people in her life had left her here with her mother and father .

She looked up at the ceiling and tried making the shadows look like her dog Billy who was now her only friend. She heard her mother shout her name "Helga, Helga, get down here now, we have to go to market". She reluctantly swung her legs out of the bed... "Another day in paradise"she thought.

Helga's mother, Greta, was a timid woman who always done what her husband told her to do so she didn't get a slap, but even when she obeyed Ralph she still got punished for something. He Just seemed to get pleasure from hurting her. Greta was a dressmaker. She sold the things she made at market on a Saturday and took in neighbours alterations and repaired items during the week to make enough money to survive.They had several chickens and Helga's job was to collect the eggs and sell them at the market. Between them they managed to make enough money to put food on the table and supply enough alcohol for Ralph, who spent his days sleeping and the evenings drinking heavily. There also had to be enough money to pay for Ralph's lady friends at the brothel above the pub. Greta and Helga always breathed a sigh of relief when Ralph went out in the evening because when he was drunk he often became loud and abusive which would usually escalate to a full blown violent situation where her mother was beaten and Helga was sent to her bedroom where She would put her fingers in her ears to block out the sound of her mother's crying and begging her father to stop.

They done well at the market and on the way home bought some food , Ralph's beer and there was enough left for Helga to buy a new ball for Billy.

That afternoon Helga wrapped a shawl around her shoulders and took Billy for a walk to the base of the mountain where she introduced him to his new ball . Billy was chasing his new toy and they were both happy. After awhile she realised how cold it had become. She didn't want to go home because she knew her father would be drunk. Maybe he had gone into town to see one of his lady friends she thought ,but decided not to go home just yet. She walked a little further up the mountain to the old barn where she laid on a bale of hay and snuggled up to Billy with her shawl over the both of them.She smiled as she thought of Walter. If she was older she could have gone with her sister, new brother in law and Walter to the city. Maybe she could go when she turned 15 But that was over a year away. Until then she was stuck in the small town where she had no friends. She was lonely. She wanted to be loved.

Helga thought of the good times she had spent with her sister. They were very close. As she laid there thinking , the good memories turned to the bad. She remembered her fathers heavy hand on both her mother and Anna and the screaming and begging for it to stop. Helga forced herself to think of the good things.

A noise awoke her from her daydreaming. There were people talking, approaching the barn. She sat up and looked straight into the face of Hector and then Igor, two boys who were in her class at school .

Helga felt uncomfortable and got up to leave. Hector stood in front of her and blocked her path. Billy growled. Don't go Hector said. We want to be your friend. She sat down again and listened to the boys telling jokes and laughing. She began to relax and joined in the conversation. Then Igor sat beside her and put his arm around her. I like you he said, will you give me a kiss. Her heart skipped a beat, she had never kissed anyone before. She had almost kissed Walter once but had backed away because she was shy. Igor leaned forward and kissed her on the lips. She got up quickly, gave a girly giggle and said "I'll see you here tomorrow".She ran out of the barn with Billy behind her. She looked back up at the barn and the two boys gave her a wave. She waved back. Her heart was racing, a boy liked her! A boy kissed her !

Chapter Two

As she almost reached home it started to snow. It was that wet snow that melted as soon as it touched the ground. In a few short minutes she was soaked through to the skin and shivery cold.

The house was quiet, She crept into the house to find Greta at her sewing machine. Her father was not home. Her mother told her to get out of her wet clothes before she caught a chill. As she stood naked in front of the mirror she looked at her body. She had small breasts and pubic hair down below. She was almost a young woman.

She got dressed and went back downstairs and asked her mother if she could have a bra. Her mother laughed and said not to be silly as she didn't have anything to put in a bra yet.

Seeing the disappointment in her daughters

face she said she would try and make her one that evening ,But first she needed to do a big job. Because it was snowing very hard Greta was worried that Ralph would get wet on his way home from his visit to the pub and told Helga to take an umbrella to her father. She was given instructions to go into the pub from the back entrance and up the stairs. Her father would be in one of the rooms with a lady friend. She would see his coat outside the door and was to leave the umbrella there and then return back home.

Helga followed her mother's instructions and she soon arrived at the pub. She looked in the window and she could see lots of men inside. Someone was playing a piano. She went round the back of the pub , in the door and up the stairs. She walked along the corridor looking for her father's coat. She could hear lots of grunts and groans and girls giggling. She spotted her father's coat and as she laid the umbrella beside it she noticed the door was ajar and she saw her father naked on a bed with a naked lady squatting on his face. Helga froze... she could not stop looking. She didn't quite know what they were doing but they were both enjoying it. She suddenly looked away and quickly made her way home. Her mother was in bed when she got home so she also went to bed. She lay awake for a long time thinking about Igor's kiss and thinking about what she saw her father doing with that lady.

It was Sunday morning. She could hear her father snoring and her mother's sewing machine humming. She went downstairs to talk to her mother. She wanted to know what her father had been doing with that lady.She got on well with her mother and found it easy to talk to her. Her mother continued sewing but listened to Helga's questions. Greta told Helga about sex and what men liked. Men loved to have sex and receive pleasure and it was a natural function for adults to enjoy. Then she stopped sewing and excitedly stood up and gave Helga the item she had been sewing . It was a bra, more of a bodice, but nice. Her mother helped her put it on. It fitted her lovely. Greta told her to go look in the mirror, as she looked a proper young lady. Just as she went to go up the stairs her father came into the room. "What the hell have you got on" he roared at her. "Get it off now"......... "Now.. I said". She tried to protest but it went on deaf ears "you look a slut" he said "get it off". Helga was whimpering as she tried to get the bra off without showing off her breasts. Ralph got impatient and grabbed her arm and pulled her towards him and then ripped the bra from her body. Ralph was in a rage he started throwing things around the room he pushed the sewing machine off the table. He told Helga to hold her head up and put her arms by her side so he could see her breasts. He picked up the leather strap from the sewing machine which lay on the floor and started to thrash her body repeatedly whilst calling her names. Greta was begging him to stop and was trying to pull him away from Helga who was now laying on the floor curled up in the foetal position trying to protect her body. Ralph's attention turned to Greta and he started to beat her with his fist. Helga ran upstairs grabbed her coat and ran out into the cold with Billy following behind her. She didn't stop running till she reached the barn where she laid down on the bale of hay with Billy by her side. she cried herself to sleep.

She didn't know how long she slept for but as she tried to move, every bone in her body ached. She unbuttoned her coat and looked down at her almost naked body , she was covered in bruises and weal's. She started to cry again and Billy nuzzled into her. What was she going to do.

She knew she had to go home at some stage but for now she couldn't even stand up. She started thinking about her mother and how badly she may be hurt. She had to go home now because her mother was probably in pain and also worried about her.

When she got home her father was sleeping. Her mother was in her bedroom so Helga went to her own room. She did not eat that day and spent the rest of the day and night in bed.

Monday morning. she got up to go to school. When she saw Greta in the kitchen she was shocked at her mother's bruised face, they both hugged each other and cried together. Ralph said she was to stay home from school that day and help her mother do some chores. Helga knew it was because he didn't want anyone to know what he had done but she didn't say anything. She went outside to feed the chickens and collect the eggs.

A few days later the bruises were subsiding and she didn't hurt so bad. she was allowed to go to school. She didn't like school because She had no friends. She was called scruffy and ugly by most of the kids. Today wasn't so bad and she felt a little different because Hector and Igor were her new friends.

After school that day Helga went to neighbours homes to collect work for her mother and then headed up to the barn to meet Hector and Igor. This time Igor kissed her straight away and sat with his arm around her while they talked.For awhile they were just mucking around and joking and then Igor asked Helga if she had seen a penis before. She said she had seen her father's and told the boys about what she had seen the other night. Igor unzipped his pants and pulled his penis out "look at this" he said "do you want to touch it". Hannah remembered what her mother had told her about men liking sex and she wanted to be liked by these boys."OK" She said. She put her hand on his penis and it was hard, she felt excited, her heart was beating rapidly as Igor kissed her and put his tongue in her mouth. He asked to see her vagina. She was scared but excited at the same time. she pulled her underwear down and both boys had a good look. They stopped, laughed and then decided to go home. They arranged to meet at the barn again on Saturday afternoon.

That night Helga laid -in bed thinking about what had gone on. She felt different, She was looking forward to Saturday already.Igor was going to fall in love with her and one day they would be married.

Saturday morning Helga and her mother went to market and because Ralph had broken Greta's sewing machine they had nothing to sell, only the eggs. They barely made any money and they had to spend it on beer and put a bit of money aside for Ralph's lady visits. Greta could not do any alterations until she could afford to repair the sewing machine so Helga had to return the neighbours items untouched which meant no payment. They would have to think of another way to make money.

Chapter Three

When Helga returned home from school her mother was waiting at the opened door waving a letter. " you have a letter Helga , it's from Anna " her mother exclaimed excitedly. Helga had never received a letter before and she stared at the envelope for what seemed like an eternity , before she opened it. She skimmed her eyes across the page and told her mother Anna was coming home for Christmas.

Greta was rushing around excitingly and Helga went up to her room to read her letter properly.

As she read she learnt that Anna's husband Peter had been sent to assist the German army as the war in Europe had expanded. Her sister would be bringing Walter with her to visit at Christmas.

Christmas was only a little over a week away and Greta and Helga busied themselves making decorations and preparing for the visit.Greta handmade some Christmas napkins and Helga helped her mother make pies early Saturday morning and they took them to market to sell along with the eggs and a few clothes Greta had hand sewn that week. They done well and had money to buy a gift for Anna and Walter as well as some special Christmas fare.

That afternoon she took Billy for a walk up to the barn. It started to snow hard. Eventually Hector turned up on his own. Helga was disappointed Igor was not with him. She was looking forward to kissing him and touching his penis.

Hector joked and chatted for a while and then they both decided to go home. The snow was deep and Pushing open the barn door was very hard. They were surprised at how hard it was snowing. The wind was howling and it was snowing so hard the visibility was zero. They pulled the barn door closed again and sat on a bale of hay and put Helga's shawl over the pair of them. They would have to wait until the snow storm eased before trying to go home.

Hector talked some more and Helga told him about her sister and Walter coming for Christmas. Hector asked Helga if she liked Igor more than Walter and she said she liked all boys. Hector put his arm around her and she did not push him away. She looked up at him and he pulled her closer and kissed her on her lips. His tongue was in her mouth and she felt his hand caressing one of her small breasts. He started breathing heavily as his hand went down her body and landed between her legs. She gasped as he touched her there. He took her hand and put it on his hard penis. "Do you like it ?" he asked. Helga didn't speak. She stood up and pulled her underwear down and stepped out of her knickers. She held up her skirt and said kiss me down there. I want to know if it feels nice". Hector took off his pants and Helga laid on the bale of hay with her legs opened. His penis was huge Helga thought as she gently stroked it. Hector started kissing her inner thigh.

Billy awoke from his sleep as the barn door made a loud noise. He jumped up and barked.. Hector and Helga stopped what they were doing to look up and see Helga's father staring straight at them.

"You dirty whore" Ralph bellowed.

Hector froze.

Ralph told him to get out of his sight and Hector didn't need telling twice. He pulled on his pants and ran out of the barn.

Helga was fumbling to put her underwear on as her father was shouting at her.

He told her to stop trying to put her underclothes on and to sit down on the hay. He sent the dog out of the barn and pulled the door shut.

"So you think you are a woman ?" He said.

Helga was silent and she could feel her heart beating hard in her chest.He told her to open her legs so he could see her vagina. She done as she was told.She was so frightened of what her father was going to do.

Ralph unbuckled his belt and unzipped his fly. He ordered Helga to Open her legs wider and touch her vagina as he preceded to masturbate whilst yelling obscenities at her. When Ralph was done he pulled up his pants , removed his belt and thrashed her half naked body repeatedly with the buckle hooking into her skin.

The perspiration was running from his brow when he brought the belt down for the final time. He left the barn leaving Helga sobbing with the pain he had inflicted upon her.

She must have fallen asleep as when she opened her eyes she could see daylight through the holes in the barn roof. She laid still for awhile not daring to move in anticipation of the pain she would encounter when she did. She thought through what had occurred and began to cry.

At least it had stopped snowing and she slowly walked down the mountain hurting with every step she took. Billy raced towards her as she almost reached home. His ball in his mouth, wanting to play a game. He was oblivious of what had happened to her.

Greta met her at the door and gasped at the sight of her daughters opened wounds. Ralph was out so Greta took a bowl of warm water to Helga's room and tenderly bathed her wounds and listened to her young daughters ordeal. Greta cradled Helga in her arms, feeling guilty that she was allowing this to happen.

Lucky it was school holidays leading up to Christmas and Helga was relieved she didn't have to face Hector. She felt embarrassed that her father had caught them together, she hoped he still liked her. She hoped Igor still liked her too.

Her body's aches and pains got less each day and her mind was focused on Anna and Walters visit. Helga and her mother worked hard around the house making it warm and welcoming. The night before the expected arrival Ralph stayed home and he didn't have a drink either. The house smelt like Christmas should smell ,Helga thought as she laid in her bed taking in the aroma wafting up from the kitchen. She started to doze when she was startled by her father standing over her. He sat on her bed and said " don't utter a word to your sister or Walter about what happens here girl. If you do I will break every bone in yours and your mother's body and bury you along with your beloved dog'.

Helga looked up at the station clock. The train was due in 10 minutes. She was so excited. From the corner of her eye she saw a crowd gathered around the newspaper stand and wondered what the commotion was about. Greta had seen it too and they both went over to see what was going on. The newspaper headline said the war was escalating and Denmark had been drawn deeper into the conflict with many German soldiers occupying Copenhagen. Greta looked at Helga but neither said a word. They didn't have to. They were both hoping Anna would not return to the city after Christmas because it was too dangerous.

The train pulled into the station and they waited for their guests to embark. When Helga spotted Anna she had to do a double check. Anna was expecting a baby!

Walter trailed behind carrying the bags and when he saw Helga he dropped them and ran to her with open arms. They hugged one another extremely tight and she felt a warm glow. She was so happy to see them both.

On the tram ride back to town Anna told them she was five months pregnant and was very happy, in good health and excited at becoming a mother.

Then she became sad. She was sad because Peter had been taken to Berlin by the Germans to assist them and he did not know they were having a child. Greta reassured her he would know soon enough and this was great news.

Chapter four

Christmas was a happy time in the house. Ralph was behaving the perfect father. Helga watched her father fuss around her sister as if she was a porcelain doll. She was not jealous , but she wished she had that kind of relationship with her father. Helga knew Anna had received many a good beating at the hands of Ralph but now they seemed to get along. Maybe her father would be better towards her when she became older she thought to herself.

Walter was very handsome but the six months he had been away had changed him ,he seemed old for his 15 years, and she suddenly realised he was almost a man, almost old enough to marry and have a family. Helga noticed there was a distance between them and not only by miles.

One afternoon Anna and Helga had a chance to spend sometime together and took a walk up towards the mountain. Anna said she hadn't been to the barn in years, in fact since they were little kids. "Come on" she said."let's go have a look".

Helga stopped walking and said "no , Anna, I can't go in there".

Helga had an awful feeling creep over her body when she thought of the last time she was in the barn a week ago. The pain in her limbs had gone but the thoughts of her father kept reappearing in her head.

"what's wrong Helga" ? Anna asked her sister.

Helga sat down on a wet rock and cried uncontrollably and her sister put her arm around her shoulder to comfort her. After she calmed down she told her sister everything. Anna listened with tears falling down her cheeks. When Helga had finished talking she looked into her sisters eyes searching for a response. Anna dabbed her sisters eyes with her handkerchief and then dabbed her own. She stood up and lifted her skirt to show Anna her healing weal's on her legs. Anna stared a few seconds but said nothing. She slowly raised her own skirt and bared her own scars. Anna had encountered the same treatment from their father when she was 13 years old. Anna told her that her father used to touch her breasts and vagina when she was alone with him. When she got older it had suddenly stopped. Anna gasped as the realisation hit her. The reason he had stopped was because Helga was to take her place. They held each other tight and comforted each other. Helga had known Anna had received beatings from their father but not to the same extent as her, and she had no idea about the sexual advances Anna had endured.

The next few days passed by fast and it was soon time for Anna and Walter to leave. Greta tried to persuade them to stay because of the situation in Copenhagen. She begged but didn't succeed as Anna said her life was in the city now and she needed to be there when Peter returned from Berlin. Helga spent an hour with Walter and they talked. He said he had a girlfriend in Copenhagen. Helga was sad but understood that things had changed and she was to focus her attention on Igor, or maybe Hector.

Anna told Helga to be strong and as soon as things got better in the city and after the baby was born she would have Helga live with her in the city. Greta cried uncontrollably as the train left the station. She was frightened for Anna's safety. Helga had mixed feelings as she didn't know what was the most scariest … bombings or her father.

After Anna and Walter left Helga clung to the words her sister had promised. She was to keep her head down and bide the time she could leave the town and her awful existence.She also hoped Peter was safe and the war would be over soon.

In February Ralph got arrested by German military officials for behaving drunk and disorderly in the town.Whilst he was in the town jail Helga and Greta had been dancing around the kitchen feeling their anxiety lift because the ogre in their life was not going to be around for sometime. Sadly for them he was beaten badly by the Nazis and sent home and not detained as they had hoped.

Helga was woken during that night by her mother's screams. Her father was swearing and yelling at her mother. She went to the top of the stairs and looked over the bannister. Her mother was on the kitchen table and her father was grunting on top of her. She could see her fathers bare buttocks moving up and down very fast as he had his hand over her mother's mouth stifling her protests for him to stop. She went back to bed and laid looking up at the shadows cast across the ceiling. All she could see was ugly faces looking down on her.

The next morning Greta told Helga her father was in a rage because the Germans had beaten him. Greta said she was disappointed he wasn't going away and they wouldn't be getting a reprieve. Helga thought maybe if he was sick he might die and it would save them for ever and then she felt guilty for thinking that and dismissed it from her mind.

Life continued in its usual pattern. School, market, good days, bad days and really horrible days.She remained friends with Igor and Hector but she had not returned to the barn since the incident with her father.

It was her fourteenth birthday and summer was upon them. She arranged to meet

Hector and Igor at the lake that afternoon to have a swim after school. Greta had made her a bathing suite out of an old tablecloth and she put it on under her dress and left the house with Billy running off ahead of her. When she got to the lake the boys were already in the water. Helga took off her dress and jumped in . Billy followed in behind her. They laughed and played ball games most of the afternoon and when the sun started to go down they decided it was time to get out of the water and head home. When they were standing on the grass sharing the one towel Igor had brought with him Hector looked at Hannah and said " your swimsuit is see through , I can see your erect nipples pointing at me" He put his hand on her breast and gently squeezed and then leaned forward and kissed her mouth. That afternoon she became a woman. She had been so aroused she let hector have his way with her while Igor watched. It was a painful experience having a erect penis inside her but also a nice feeling.

That night Helga was happy. she laid on her bed thinking of marrying Hector and having his children. She was in love and Hector loved her. Sex made men happy, and she liked it.

Chapter Five

At school on Monday Helga felt everyone was looking at her . Some of the girls in her class were sniggering and whispering. When she saw Hector she ran up to him and kissed him on the cheek. Everyone started laughing and Hector pushed her away. " Get away from me you filthy whore" he snarled at her. Helga turned to Igor but he looked the other way as if he hadn't seen her. One of the girls said "we know what you done with Hector on Saturday, you flaunted yourself at him and you gave him sex . That's what sluts do Helga". She looked at Hector for support but he said she was easy and nice girls would have said no. Helga ran out of the school in tears. She couldn't go home so she went up to the barn. She didn't go in but sat down and leaned back against the door and let the tears run freely as she tried to make sense of what was happening. She had given herself to Hector because she thought it would make him happy. Her mother had told her sex makes men happy, she thought Hector would love her and they would be married.

When she went home her father was waiting for her. She knew what was coming as her mother was trying to get between them and was telling Ralph to calm down. He was shouting and swearing about hearing from one of his lady friends that Helga had been giving one of the local boys sex. He was furious.

She ran up the stairs but he pushed Greta out of the way and reached the bedroom the same time as Helga. He pushed her down on the bed and and tore at her dress. Helga was whimpering and begging her father not to hurt her. He was in a rage. He told her to get naked whilst he was unbuckling his pants. She thought he was going to beat her but he didn't. He stripped naked and sat on the bed. He asked her if she had sucked Hectors penis and she shook her head, horrified at such a thought. Ralph demanded her to get on her knees between his legs and he was going to teach her how to please a man with her mouth so she could be a proper whore. He grabbed Helga's hair and pulled her head towards his erect penis." Open your mouth wide you whore " he said.

After the act Helga was coughing and spluttering, spitting the semen out of her mouth. "That wasn't too bad" Ralph said, " I think you've done that before you lying slut"

Helga tried telling him she hadn't but he didn't listen. She felt a sharp pain as he slapped her in the side of her head. He then repeatedly began thrashing her with the buckle end of his belt. Helga recalled her mother coming into the room and begging him to stop. He pushed Greta out of the door and she fell down the stairs. Ralph continued to thrash Helga until she blacked out.

The only consolation of being beaten was she didn't have to attend school. Greta was covered in bruises but insisted she had fallen down the stairs. Helga knew her mother was frightened.

A letter arrived from Anna. She had delivered a baby boy. Helga was elated to hear some good news. Greta and Ralph were proud grandparents and although they never attended church they decided to go that coming Sunday to announce the news to the congregation.

The church was full and Helga felt safe. After the service Ralph told the congregation about the new arrival and he was telling everyone how proud he was of his lovely daughter. Helga stared at him while he was talking and she thought what a bastard he was. After his speech Helga said she would like to say something. She knew what she had to do and would have to deal with the consequences. She stood in front of the congregation and slowly raised her dress. Everyone was silent. She raised it higher and people started to gasp. She was showing them all the fresh weal's and older scars on her young body."my father did this" she said.

The police were called and Ralph was taken to the police station for questioning. Helga and Greta went home. Now they had to wait and see what the outcome would be. The police visited their home that evening and asked lots of questions which both Greta and Helga both gave truthful answers to.

Ralph was charged for a string of offences and no bail was offered.

A few weeks went by and Ralph was sentenced to two years in gaol for the attacks on both women. It was not enough thought Helga but better than him getting a non custodial punishment. At least they could breathe easier for awhile.

Greta became unwell, Helga thought it may have had something to do with the stress she was going through but whatever the reason, it wasn't good. She spent most days in bed. Her cough was on her chest and she rattled with each breath. Helga stayed at home and took care of her mother and done the chores. It was better than school. There was no money coming in and they were living on eggs.

Greta was taken to the hospital when she began coughing up blood.The doctor told Helga her mother was very sick and she had something called tuberculosis. Helga wrote to Anna to tell her the news but she didn't receive a reply. Helga was told by the authorities that she was too young to stay at the house on her own and her grandmother from her fathers family had become her temporary guardian.

Helga was taken to another town several miles away to stay with her grandma and two uncles. She had never met them before and they had merely been mentioned to her. Helga felt uneasy when she met her new found family. Her father was the image of his mother and the uncles were both overweight men with bad manners .

It wasn't long before She realised that it wasn't only her fathers looks he had inherited from his mother. She was a nasty lady. She sat in a armchair all day smoking one cigarette after the other whilst the uncles done everything. When she yelled at them they jumped and done what they were told promptly. That surprised Helga as they were both tough looking men in their forties and looked scary.

The farm kept them busy and Helga went to the local school week days so she didn't really see much of them.

She had her own bedroom and it was warm and cosy. She had been allowed to bring Billy with her and he was allowed to sleep in her room. Winter was coming and it was great having Billy to snuggle up to, to keep warm.

Grandma was loud and swore a lot at the boys but she was OK with Helga. But that was about to change.

Chapter Six

One Saturday evening Helga was in the sitting room writing letters. One to the hospital inquiring about her mother and another to her sister. She was concerned as she had not heard from Anna since the baby was born. She had written but never had a reply. Maybe she had moved house she wondered.

She could hear her grandma talking with her uncle Rufus in the kitchen. "Can you lend me some money cos I want to go into town tonight to pick up a woman, I'm sex starved" he said. "No, I am not giving you money to waste on a whore when you have what you need right here"she yelled back it him.

Helga knew what she meant straight away and her heart missed a beat. Grandma was referring to Helga ,telling Rufus to take what he needed from his niece !

That night she laid in bed wide awake. Billy laid beside her. She listened and waited for Rufus to come in and get what he wanted. She didn't sleep at all through fear but surprisingly he didn't enter her room. She gave a big sigh of relief and got dressed and went downstairs early that next morning.

Saturday's she helped out on the farm by feeding the animals. They had several cows and sheep and three beautiful horses. Helga put some fruit in a sack , put it on the barrow and headed up to the stables to feed the horses. She spent a couple of hours brushing them and talking to them. This was the highlight of her week. As she was leaving the stable Rufus appeared in the doorway "don't go yet" he said. Helga was scared but she tried to remain calm by making general conversation. He pushed her against the door and started to kiss her neck . She could feel his hot breath and feel his hard penis pushing against her. "I'm going to make you feel good and you are going to make me feel good too" he said as his hands were grabbing at her breasts over the top of her clothes. He stood back and told her to tell him she wanted him. She was so scared. "I want you" she whispered. She stood rigid as he slowly undone her buttons and removed her blouse. Her small breasts where firm and as he touched her nipples they became erect. He placed his mouth over a nipple and flicked it with his tongue. Helga was getting aroused. She knew she shouldn't but she couldn't help it....

That evening while Helga was out walking with Billy she kept going over what had happened with Rufus earlier that day. She felt elated. Rufus had been so gentle with her and had made her feel good. Sex could be beautiful and she could understand why her mother had told her men liked sex. She liked it too.

Sex with Rufus became a regular thing, neither could get enough of each other's body. Sometimes they shared Rufus's bed and made love all night long and sometimes they would grab a quick rough 10 minutes during the day. She never really talked to Rufus, It was a mutual sexual bond they shared and both were content with the pleasure they gave each other. Rufus may have been overweight and not very appealing but he knew how to please a woman.

She had been at her grandma's house for six months when news came that her mother had passed away. Uncle Robert and Uncle Rufus accompanied Helga to the funeral. They were the only people in attendance. Helga was hoping Anna would be there but she probably did not know of their mother's passing. That night they stayed in the old house. Helga burst into tears as she sat at her mother's sewing machine which was still broken and some good and bad memories came flooding back. She held the sewing machine belt in her hand and turned to her uncles. She needed to tell someone about her ordeal with her father. They listened and Rufus comforted her. She felt safe. It was the first time in a very long time she had felt any affection towards her. She knew it wasn't love but it was a nice feeling.

Back at grandma's house time passed by quickly. She was now 15 and had finished school. She worked on the farm at weekends and during the week she worked a few hours a day at the local store. Her sexual desires were still being met by Rufus and life wasn't to bad.

One evening while having dinner grandma casually said " Ralph has been freed from prison and he is coming here to stay with us because the house in Roskilde is empty now Greta has passed and he needs to be with his family". Helga's heart skipped a beat and she looked at Rufus. He put his hand over hers as a gesture to say it will be OK.

Then grandma continued "looks like you will have to share Helga now Rufus" and gave a wink. Helga ran out of the house and Billy followed her. But Rufus didn't.

Chapter Seven

The day Ralph arrived everyone was friendly. Ralph looked at his daughter and smiled " you've turned out a good looking woman" he said. " I bet your knickers are off more than they are on" and they all looked at her and laughed. Grandma told Ralph that Rufus had been giving it to her to keep her happy. Helga left the room.

A few weeks went by and things weren't too bad with Ralph around. She continued to have sex with uncle Rufus and it was an unspoken normal.

It was Roberts birthday and they all went to the pub in town to celebrate except for Helga. She spent her time writing another letter to Anna. She left the Envelope blank as she didn't know where to send it and put it in her top draw on top of the pile she had previously written.

The family returned and they were all drunk.

Even grandma was singing rude ditty's. Helga was called downstairs by her father. "Give us some entertainment girl" he shouted at her. She began to sing and they all clapped along laughing and joining in. Helga was given some whiskey and she quite liked it . She liked the way being tipsy made her relax. She began to have fun. The party went on for some time and grandma and Rufus both fell asleep. Helga went up to bed happy.

During the night she felt Rufus get in bed beside her and start kissing her neck. It felt good. His hand went between her legs and he rubbed her until she was wet. She pushed her bottom back and lifted a leg so he could insert his hard penis inside her. He pounded her grunting and groaning until they both reached their climax together. She fell asleep content.

When she was at the stable that afternoon feeding the horses Robert came up beside her and made small talk about the horses. They chatted for awhile and he stroked her hair. She stepped back. She was a little surprised as he had not shown her any attention before. He lent forward and kissed her on the cheek. "Thank you for last night" he whispered. She looked at him in shock. Then the realisation hit her that Robert was in bed with her last night and not Rufus. Robert pulled her to him and kissed her passionately. Helga responded by undoing his fly and releasing his penis. She wanted it now. He laid back on a hay bale while she took her underwear off and straddled him and rode him like a stallion. She was loving it. Sex is wonderful she thought.

Now she was having sex with both uncles. She didn't feel bad about it because everybody was happy. She was liking her new life.

An official letter arrived one morning addressed to Ralph. He read it at the kitchen table and Helga saw a tear roll down his cheek. She had never seen her father show that emotion before and she guessed it was bad news. Ralph threw the letter on the table and then stormed out the back door. Grandma picked up the letter and read it.she looked at Helga and said "Anna and her child have been killed in an air raid in Copenhagen"

Helga went to her room and sobbed uncontrollably. She would never see her sister again and never meet her nephew.

Ralph came home from the pub that night. He had lost a child and a grandchild he was devastated even though their relationship hadn't been normal. He continued drinking well into the night whilst the rest of the house was sleeping.

Helga was woken by the smell of her fathers alcohol breath on her face. She froze as he fumbled with her nightdress trying to lift it and pull her legs apart. "Come on Helga" he said " give some sex to your father. You like to share your body with the family". As he tried to penetrate her she was pushing him off and he was getting angry. He lifted his fist and punched her in the face and she sobbed as she felt the blood trickle down the back of her throat. Billy was at the bottom of the bed growling at Ralph . Ralph was getting more angry as he was trying to prise Helga's legs apart. Suddenly Ralph let out a high pitched scream . Billy had bitten him on the thigh and a big chunk was dangling by a thread. Billy's barking and Ralph yelling had woken the whole household. Grandma assisted Ralph out of the bedroom to tend to his injured leg

The next day Helga went to work at the store. She made conversation with the customers and blocked the previous nights ordeal from her mind.

After work she called Billy to go for a walk. He didn't come to her when she called so she went outside to look for him. The vision in front of her eyes made her physically sick.

Billy was hanging from the washing line with a cord around his neck. She tried frantically to cut him free but he was already dead. Her father had killed her dog.

That night she decided to leave. She could not stay near her father any longer.

Chapter Eight

Arriving in Copenhagen with knowing no one and having no money was frightening . Helga roamed the streets asking if there was any work with accommodation. She slept rough a few nights in shop doorways and scavenged food from trash cans for survival. Eventually she went into a church and although she had not prayed for a long time she knelt at the alter and prayed to the lord to help her. A hand rested on her shoulder and when she looked up she saw a nun smiling down at her.
Helga was given a job at the hospital which was run by the nuns. She was offered to train as a nurse which she accepted eagerly. She was given a small room at the top of the building which she shared with another trainee nurse called Catherine. She was happy she had landed on her feet. A good job and a roof over her head was all she needed right now.

Work was hard at the hospital and she worked long hours. She was so tired at the end of her shifts she would just sleep finding a little time during the day to eat. The nuns were very strict but she didn't mind. Catherine was a rebellious girl and would sneak out at night to go to parties and see her boyfriend. When she got caught sneaking back in the nuns would punish her by rapping her knuckles with a wooden spoon until they bled and then pour malt vinegar over her hands to inflict intense pain. Of course that meant she couldn't have shifts in the hospital so received no pay for the days she didn't work. She was always asking Helga if she could borrow money. Helga always obliged as she never spent her wages. She thought the nuns were nasty. Especially being religious.

Helga's hard work was rewarded by promoting her to theatre nurse. She loved caring for the patients and received good job satisfaction. The only thing she disliked about the job was Mr Morley the chief surgeon. He gave her the creeps with his leering at all the nurses.

It was her day off and she decide to venture out to the city to buy a few clothes. She was shocked at how bad the place had been devastated by bombings. Several of the shops she remembered were now piles of rubble. She enjoyed the shopping trip and was pleased with the dress and shoes she had bought. She realised she was hungry and went into the station café to buy a sandwich. As she was studying the menu she was overcome by the feeling that someone was looking at her. She slowly looked up and scanned the café. She stopped and stared right into the eyes a young man who was staring back at her. "Helga" he mouthed "Walter" she mouthed back. They both stood up and rushed towards each other meeting in the centre of the café. Helga threw her arms around his neck and he kept repeating her name " Helga, Helga, Helga"

The pair became inseparable from then on.

She learnt Walter had trained to be an electrician and had moved around Denmark, feeling very fortunate he had not been harmed in any air raids.He revealed the girlfriend he had told Helga about was not true and he had thought it would be easier for her to forget about him if she thought he had someone else.

He told how he found out he was from German blood and his father was high up in the German army. He felt blessed he's mother had brought him to Denmark when he was a baby.

She learnt that Walter had planned to go on a cycling trip around Australia and he was booked to go in two weeks. He would be gone for many months and Walter told Helga he wanted to marry her when he returned. Hannah was overjoyed at the idea of being Mrs Carling and hopefully have a lot of little Carlings running around her ankles.

Helga met Walters travelling partner and was very impressed . He was a good looking boy and very friendly. She knew they would have an exciting time and Yuri promised he would bring Walter back safe and well.

Helga was happy. She pushed the thoughts of her ugly past out of her mind and concentrated on her work. She was always tired because of the long hours in theatre and hardly went out. Catherine was still always out in the evening and always getting punished by the nuns.

One night after Helga finished work she went up to her room. She was so tired she fell asleep on top of her bed.

A noise awoke her and she thought it was Catherine returning. She rubbed her eyes and sat up on the bed to see Mr Morley the chief surgeon was masturbating in her wardrobe . When he saw she was awake the hurried out of the room dropping something on his way. Helga was dazed and shocked at what she had just witnessed. She picked up what Mr Morley had dropped in his haste and stared down at her new dress she had bought a few weeks ago .. sticky with semen.

She avoided Mr Morley from then on . She refused shifts and pretended she was sick so she didn't have to work with him. The nuns weren't happy and she was punished by having her meals minimised and her knuckles rapped with a wooden spoon for telling fibs about the respectable Mr Morely.

She applied for another job at the maternity hospital and accepted a position as a trainee midwife. She found lodgings with a nice family near the hospital and made a good friend of the daughter who was named Frances. Helga had to study so would go to the library at the weekends to read for her exams. It was then she learnt about periods. She had never been told woman had periods and why. She realised she had never had one. Something was wrong.

Helga confided in Frances who was very supportive and went to the doctors with her. Helga was told after several tests that she would probably never be a mother and she was absolutely devastated.

She continued to work and study and assisted delivering babies. She loved her job it was the happiest she had ever been. At night she would lie awake questioning if it was her fault she could not have a child of her own.

She would go to the library and read books about infertility and the woman's body. She was looking for hope.

She thought about Walter returning from Australia and if he would still wish to marry her if he knew she would probably never give him a child.

Walter had been away for along time. Maybe he had met another woman in Australia she wondered. Winter came and went and she had heard no word from Walter. Helga began to think he wasn't coming back. She continued going to the library and become friends with a man named Tomas. They started meeting in the evenings and she would go to his house and have passionate sex with him. She pushed Walter out of her mind. Tom gave her so much pleasure she saw him nearly every night.

Helga passed her exam to become a qualified midwife when she was 18 years old. It was 1945 and the war was over. Celebrating the end of the war and her qualification Helga and Tom went to a party and drank lots of champagne. That night she had sex with both Tom and her friend

Frances. Helga's first threesome was one of many. Frances and Helga started sharing their bed at the family home. Helga learnt sex was beautiful with women as well as men. She was feeling loved.

Helga finished her shift at the hospital and went to Tomas home. She was ready for a night of passion. Tomas was in bed so Helga undressed and slipped in beside him. She kissed his neck and massaged his shoulders and awoke him from his sleep by gently stroking his penis. She wanted him inside her. Tomas obliged and pounded into her.

Giving her multiple orgasms. She fell asleep in his arms.

The next morning Tomas acted differently towards her. She could sense something was not quite right. "What's wrong Tomas" she asked. He looked her in the eyes and said "I'm sorry Helga, but the time has come for us to stop our encounters. I am going to marry Frances, she is expecting our baby"

Helga felt the blood drain from her body. She thought he loved her and he would marry her. She felt she was being punished for something because nothing ever worked out they way she wanted it to. Helga left Tomas home and went back to her lodgings she had been sharing with Frances and packed her bags.

Chapter Nine

Being back in Roskilde was strange at first but she soon became settled. It was good living by herself in the old house. The good memories made her happy and the bad memories were pushed out of her mind. She got a job in the local store where she had worked before and life was bearable.

She had met up with Igor a few times and she liked him a lot. She was now 20 years old. She yearned to be married. Walter had not returned and she thought that she was wasting her life waiting for him because he may not ever come back. She thought long and hard about Igor being her husband, but she dare not tell him she could not have children.

One evening Igor called at her home for supper. Helga was teasing him by getting his hand and placing it on her thigh throughout the meal. After she had washed the dishes she sat next to him on the couch and lifted her skirt to show him she was not wearing underwear. She placed his hand on her breast. They began kissing passionately and quickly became naked and had sex on the couch. It was good.

Igor couldn't keep away from her after that night. Every opportunity they were having sex. Helga wanted Igor to ask her to marry him but he didn't. They went for long walks holding hands and talking about their dreams. He never mentioned marriage or children .

Helga was working at the store one day when she got terrible stomach cramps. When she got home the pain was getting worse. She went to the toilet and was shocked when she saw blood in her underwear. After a visit to the doctor it was confirmed she had started her menstrual cycle. She was elated that whatever had been wrong with her had righted itself and there was no reason why she didn't have a chance to conceive a child. She continued to see Igor and they continued to have sex regularly. One night Helga got the courage to ask Igor if he ever wanted children. "Yes " he replied "one day in the future when I'm married".

Helga didn't continue the conversation.

She laid on her bed looking at the ceiling making patterns with the shadows, as she often did, and came to the conclusion that Igor was not in love with her. They enjoyed their time together and had fun. Life was good but there was something missing. She knew his mother didn't like them seeing each other as Helga had the reputation of being a slut in the town for being free with the boys when she was younger. Nobody knew she was desperate to be loved.

After a few regular periods she missed one.

When she told Igor she must be pregnant he didn't hesitate to ask her to marry him as he said it was the right thing to do. Igor never told his family and Helga had no one to tell. All Helga's dreams had come true,she was to be married and have a child. She was very happy.

They travelled to Copenhagen and used two strangers as witnesses to their marriage. They spent two weeks in the city and enjoyed their time together. They talked about returning to the city to have the baby and live their married life there.

They kept their marriage a secret from Igor's family until they returned to Roskilde husband and wife.

Igor's mother was not happy as she knew Helga was the young whore who was talked about by many. Now she was her daughter-in- law. She was horrified and told them both she was disappointed and didn't want anything to do with them . "Are you sure the baby is yours" she asked Igor. He didn't answer and walked out of his mother's house.

The pair set up home together in Helga's family home.

A few weeks after the wedding Helga started to bleed. She was taken to the hospital and after examination was told she had not been pregnant. She had been late for a period.

Igor was disappointed and very angry and his parents were livid. "The whore had tricked their son into marrying her". Igor's father exclaimed to his wife. "She was a liar" his mother retorted. Igor thought they were right, he had been tricked. He felt both disappointed and humiliated and went back to live with his family. Helga was alone in her home. She had genuinely thought she was going to have a baby.She felt ashamed to go to work or even be seen out by the townsfolk as she now knew what they thought of her.

She stayed at home and became unwell. She hardly ate and became extremely thin. She had no energy and lost interest in living. Lucky for her the lady she had worked for at the store became worried as she hadn't been seen for weeks and went to the house to investigate. She found Helga unconscious on the couch.

Helga was nursed back to health by Mrs Goldberg from the store.

When Helga was feeling stronger she decided to get her life sorted and make plans for her future. She would go back to Copenhagen and continue midwifery. She would concentrate on her work and keep men out of her life.

For two years Helga worked at the hospital

in Copenhagen she became sister in charge and loved delivering the tiny babies . She got great joy from seeing the love in the new parents eyes when they met their new babies. Helga often thought of having her own child one day but she was content helping others and sharing their joy for now.

Whilst on shift at the hospital one evening Helga had a telephone call. It was Walter.

He was in Roskilde, looking for her. Mrs Goldberg had told him where she was and he wanted to see her. Helga was surprised and delighted.

Walter had just returned from overseas and his first priority was her.

He would be in Copenhagen on Saturday.

Helga took her time getting ready to meet Walter. She wanted to look her best for him. She was excited that Walter was back in Denmark and he wanted to see her. She had not had a boyfriend since she had been in

Copenhagen because she had put everything into her career.

Walter was still very handsome and her heart skipped a beat as he came towards her. They held each other for a long time. She didn't want to let him go. Eventually they held hands and walked to the nearby café. They both had so much to say but neither said anything. Helga kept looking at Walter and she was smiling. Walter was smiling too. That afternoon they went back to the hotel Walter was staying in and went to his room. Helga wanted to kiss him and anticipated they would end up in bed. That didn't happen and she was a little disappointed although she didn't say anything.

Over the next year they saw a lot of each other and Walter told her about Australia and how wonderful it was. He also told her of other places he had visited and some of the adventures he an Yuri had had.

Helga learnt that Yuri had gone back to Australia as he had married a girl from Sydney.

Walter said he wanted to go back to Australia to live one day.

Helga didn't tell Walter about her marriage to Igor or about the incest and beatings she had received because she was afraid he would think it was all her fault and he may even think she had tricked Igor into marriage.

They continued to see each other and Walter got a electricians job in the hospital were Helga worked.

Walter had been dating Helga for well over a year but he had never tried to have sex with her. She thought she wasn't appealing enough for him. It was upsetting because if they were going to be together she wanted his affection and a baby.

One evening Helga plucked up the courage

to talk to Walter. She asked him why he didn't want sex with her.He told her he wanted to but had never done it before and he was so nervous that he would let her down. Helga told him she wanted him and that night Helga taught him how to please a woman. It was wonderful. The pair became very close and Walter asked Helga to marry him and go live in Australia. Helga had her marriage to Igor annulled and the pair were married in Copenhagen with lots of Helga's and Walters work colleagues in attendance. It was a beautiful wedding and Helga was so happy. She was 24 years old and excited for what laid ahead.

Chapter Ten

It was October 1954 and a bitterly cold morning as they stood at the dock waiting to board the liner bound for Australia.It had taken over 2 years to plan the emigration and they had saved hard to be able to have a good start in their new life. Helga was so excited for the life ahead of her, in a new country with the man of her dreams. It was a chance to start again and she vowed to lock all her bad memories away in her mind and forget them forever.

She had never been outside Denmark before and never been on a ship. It was to be 7 weeks before they arrived in Sydney and she planned to enjoy every minute of the voyage.

The first day on-board was very choppy and both Helga and

Walter were extremely seasick. lucky for Helga it passed quickly but Walter was so bad he laid on his bed day and night feeling very unwell.

Helga got fed up sitting in their tiny cabin and ventured out on deck. She looked at the horizon and was amazed at the space. There were no other ships and all she could see was the ocean. She felt separated from the life she was leaving behind.She could hear music coming from inside and went to investigate.

The dance floor was full of people dancing to the band. The atmosphere was electric. Many people were drunk. Helga got herself a drink at sat at a table close to the dance floor.She clapped her hands and sang along to the tunes she knew. Helga felt happy enjoying the start of her new adventure. She talked to many people who were all embarking on a new life in Australia.They were all as excited as she was.

The next morning she was excited to tell Walter about the people she had met and

the dancing. Walter tried to be interested but he was still feeling very nauseas and laid on his bed. Helga left the cabin on her own and joined a small group who were playing quoits. She soon learnt the game and was having such fun. One of the men in the group was very attractive and he kept looking at Helga. She kept glimpsing at him. His name was Felix. After the game Felix asked Helga to join him for a drink. They talked a lot and Helga told Felix that Walter was seasick and Felix said his wife was seasick too.

A week passed and Walter had still not felt well enough to leave their cabin. Helga had been out every day with Walter's blessing as he didn't expect her to keep cooped up in a stuffy cabin. Helga made new friends with lots of Danes who were all starting a new adventure. She spent most of her time with Felix.

During their second week on-board the ship Walter ventured out of the cabin. He was introduced to some of Helga's new friends including Felix. Walter noticed the way Felix was all over Helga and he felt a stab of jealousy. Walter brushed it aside and enjoyed a few beers and watched Helga on the dance floor.

That night in the cabin Walter undressed Helga and started kissing her eagerly. Helga responded by tugging at his pants and releasing his hard penis. She wanted him so badly. They hadn't been intimate since they had been on-board the ship and they were both highly sexed.

Walter played with her breasts whilst Helga hung them in front of his face. She lowered herself down onto him but his erection had diminished. She eagerly crawled down the bed and began performing oral sex to try arousing his limp penis. It didn't work and they both fell asleep disappointed.

The next morning Walter was sick which He put down to the motion sickness again or maybe a slight hangover.Helga put it down to way too much beer the night before.

Helga went to breakfast on her own.Felix sat at her table and talked about the night before. He asked about Walter and Helga told him he was feeling unwell again. Felix asked her to spend the day with him playing quoits and having an afternoon swim . Helga was glad of the company and accepted the invitation.

Late afternoon Helga returned to her cabin to find Walter was still in bed. The ships doctor had given him some medicine to ease the vomiting but he said he still felt unwell and very tired. Helga thought that maybe Walters poor performance in bed the previous night was because he was unwell. She got in bed beside him and snuggled into him and fell asleep.

Four weeks into the voyage and Helga was feeling deflated. She wanted Walter to make love to her but he couldn't get an erection. Helga felt unloved even though she knew Walter loved her. He had got over his sickness and was beginning to enjoy the activities on board. Felix wife Mimi was better too and the foursome spent most of their time together. Helga and Mimi became good friends and shared lots of laughter and stories from their past. Helga never mentioned her abusive upbringing because she was ashamed and made up nice memories in her head to share with Mimi.These stories were so realistic Helga almost believed them herself. She painted a picture of a loving family filled with love and happiness. She pushed the truth further back in her mind. She reinvented her past and she felt happy.

Helga and Mimi were at the hair salon and Walter and Felix were having a game of tennis on the deck.After the game the men went to the lounge and had a glass of beer. Walter needed to talk to Felix about his problem in the bedroom.He was embarrassed but needed to get some advice. He told Felix his problem and Felix said it had happened to him once before but it only lasted a short while and then returned to normal. He told Walter that worrying about it would probably make worse and to try and relax. He advised him to see a doctor if it was still a problem when they arrived in Australia.Walter felt better once he had talked to Felix.

That evening the four went to dinner and on to the big band dance to celebrate Walters birthday. They talked to another couple who told them that the lower deck , third Class was very cramped and basic and the bathrooms were shared by many passengers. Helga felt blessed she and her beloved Walter had been able to afford second class tickets.

The night was full of laughter and drinking . Even Walter was on the dance floor attempting the tango and failing to the amusement of the others. They were all very drunk when the band played the last tune and all retired to their cabins happily.

Within minutes Helga was naked and she laid on the bed waiting for Walter to seduce her. He laid on the bed beside her and put his hand between her legs. Helga gasped as his fingers explored her vagina. Suddenly he stopped and snorted. Helga laid still with his hand resting on her pubic area and listened to him snore. She was so disappointed and frustrated she got up and put her night clothes on and went up to the deck and had a good cry.

Felix was up on deck having a smoke before

he retired when he spotted Helga leaning on the rail looking out into the darkness. As he approached her he could see she was crying."Helga, what's wrong?" he asked. Helga turned and faced him with tears streaming down her face. She stepped forward and lent into him and he automatically wrapped his arms around her to comfort her. They sat on a bench and Helga asked Felix for a cigarette.She had never smoked before but had heard that a smoke could be relaxing. Felix lit a cigarette and passed it to her and she took a deep draw which made her cough and splutter. She began to laugh and told Felix it was the first time she had tried a cigarette . He laughed too. After a few more draws she started to enjoy it. They went inside and found a lounge bar opened where they decided to have a night cap. Helga felt comfortable with Felix and told him she was upset because of Walter letting her down in the bedroom. Felix told her that Walter had confided in him about his problem which surprised her as she didn't think he would have admitted he had a problem. They finished their drink and when they said goodnight Felix lent in and kissed Her on the mouth. Helga pushed her lips onto his and they kissed each other passionately.They were both breathing heavily, Felix whispered in her ear come with me. She held his hand as he led her down to the lower deck and into one of the communal bathrooms.He locked the door and they both eagerly got undressed whilst kissing and touching each other. Helga looked at his body . She was so excited as he sat on the toilet with his massive erection waiting for her to straddle him and lower herself onto him. They both moaned as he entered her and she started to ride him. "I've wanted you for weeks " he said as she was going up and down on him. It was over so quickly but Helga was elated, completely satisfied, and she knew Felix was too.

For the next week they shared a cigarette, night cap and each other's body. Helga was loving it. She felt no guilt as Walter couldn't give it to her and she needed it. Mimi had told her that her sex life was great so Helga didn't think she was taking anything away from her either. So all was good.

It was Christmas Eve and they were coming to the end of their voyage. A Christmas themed party was being held that night and Mimi and Helga went to the hair salon together whilst the men went to play poker. After the girls had their hair done they went and had a cup of tea. One of the young service boys came and sat at their table and Mimi introduced him to Helga. His name was Hans. Mimi confided in Helga that she had been meeting him for fun In the evenings. Helga was shocked, she had no idea Mimi would do such a thing and especially with a boy who was so young.Helga promised she would say nothing.

Mimi said she was going below deck and asked Helga to go with her. The three went to the boys cabin and Mimi and Hans had oral sex. Helga picked up a newspaper and looked down at it

Pretending to read as she didn't know where else to look. She felt embarrassed and a little excited about being in the room. When they had finished Hans asked Helga if she wanted him to give her an orgasm but she declined.

Back on deck they joined their partners and nothing more was said.

The party that evening was wonderful. The food was good , the carol singing was beautiful and Helga was happy Walter had danced with her. when they went to bed that night Walter maintained an erection and made love to her for an hour. She was so happy.

Christmas Day was their last day on-board.

Helga ,Walter, Mimi and Felix spent the day together enjoying the company. None of them had any idea where they were heading in Australia so there was no way they could stay in touch. Saying goodbye was a bitter sweet moment but they all took memories away with them.

As She boarded the bus Helga looked back and caught a glimpse of Felix with his arm around his wife. She smiled and hoped their new life in Australia would bring them closer together.

Chapter Eleven

Sydney was hot, very hot and Helga loved the feeling of the sun on her skin.The weather was such a contrast to what she had been used to in Denmark. The first thing she wanted to buy was a swimsuit but she knew she would never wear one because of all the scars on her body.

Walter had friends in Liverpool, a Sydney suburb and he counted himself extremely lucky that they were invited to stay with the family until they found their feet.Alice and Raymond had two children who Helga was thrilled to look after to give their pregnant mother a break. Walter was out looking for work every day at the crack of dawn and he landed a job really quickly with a mining company in far North Queensland .

Helga didn't want him to go because it was 3 weeks away and 1 week home. But Walter said it was good money and he would only do the job short term to give them a good start. Before he left they found a small rental property a few streets from Alice and Raymond so it would be easy for Helga to look after the children until she could find a job in a hospital .

Helga loved the children and when the new baby was born she spent more time with Alice. She told Alice she yearned for a baby but with Walter working away her chances were slim. She didn't mention Walter had a problem with erection which made her chance of becoming pregnant near impossible. Helga blocked her wanting a child from her mind and enjoyed every minute with the ones she was looking after. She applied for jobs at hospitals and clinics in the area but had no luck.

Eventually Walter quit the job in Queensland when he was offered a job at a local electrical company. It was less wages but Helga got a job as a machinist at a factory.The two wages made up for Walters one wage from the mines but at least they were together.

"We need to talk" Helga said one night when they were in bed. "I love you with all my heart, but I want a baby and you have a problem that is stopping that from happening. What can we do Walter?" His eyes watered and a tear rolled down his cheek as he took her face in his hands. " I think about it all the time Helga, I want to be a father , I want us to have a family to make our life complete I will see a doctor , I promise'

Helga snuggled into him and cried herself to sleep.

Walter visited a doctor but Helga didn't ask him what was said. Sex was certainly more satisfying and Walter always made sure she reached a climax. But there was no penetration .

Both continued to work long hours and they saved their money to put a down payment on a new house. Alice and Raymond often visited with the children and Helga and Walter loved having them over. Walter decided to build a swimming pool in the backyard for the kids. He got some friends from work to help him at weekends and although it took months to build the finished project was perfect. The children loved it. They even had their school friends over for pool parties. Weekends were happy times for them all.

One morning Walter woke up with a raging erection"Helga ,I have a surprise" he shouted. When Helga saw his penis she quickly pulled her knickers off and climbed on top of him. She bounced up and down on him, the feeling was wonderful. Their love making lasted an hour and she felt him ejaculate inside her.

She was so happy. She prayed to god she was pregnant. Every day she didn't get her period she was more sure she was ...But she wasn't.

Walters sex drive returned and he could maintain an erection so they could indulge in sexual intercourse. Helga's need for a baby became an obsession, she thought about having a family every day. She prayed to god and cried to god.But it didn't happen. She started going to church on Sundays and read the bible every evening before bed. She started thinking about the sex she had indulged in with her uncles and the abuse from her father. She believed god was punishing her for her past and begged his forgiveness. On the outside Helga gave the impression she was happy and on the inside she was hurting so bad.

Life was good in Sydney. Walter liked his job

and Helga had made some good friends at the factory. They had Alice and Raymond over often and when they were all together the place was full of laughter. Inside Helga was yearning for their own child.

She had given up talking about it to Walter and kept her thoughts to herself churning over and over in her head. She blamed herself , she blamed Walter. But she had no answers, Only that god was punishing her but she kept that to herself.

Walter wanted to find his dear friend Yuri but he had left his last address he had for him with no forwarding address.

Walter put a small add in the paper searching for any information on his friend.

Eventually Helga got a job in the maternity ward at the hospital and she absolutely loved it . Delivering babies and seeing the love in the new mother's eyes gave her a wonderful feeling. At least she was lucky enough to see others joy even though inside she was so envious.

One day at work she was having a casual conversation with a colleague and she was asked why she didn't have children. She had never been asked before and was unsure what to say. Helga lied and said she didn't want any as she liked her social life and freedom for her and Walter to do what they liked. She laughed it off and said she was selfish. On her way home she cried and asked herself why why why couldn't she have a baby.

"Helga, Helga, wake up" she could hear voices in the distance. "Helga, wake up"

She opened her eyes to see flames in front of her. The curtains were on fire.she choked as she took a deep breath in and the smoke it the back of her throat. She was disoriented and unaware of where she was. She tried to stand but couldn't. She faded into darkness.

Helga woke to the sound of people taking and children laughing. She opened her eyes and saw Walter , Alice and Raymond sitting at her bedside. The children were playing a game on the floor. She realised she was in a hospital bed.

Walter grabbed her hand when he saw she was awake. "Oh Helga " he said " I thought I was going to lose you"

Helga learnt that she had fallen asleep with a cigarette in her hand which had set fire to the table cloth and escalated to the curtains . Alice had seen the smoke as she rounded the corner onto the street and the fire service had been alerted. Luckily the fire-fighters got Helga out and put out the fire without the loss of the house and Helga's life. She was lucky not to receive any burns.

She thought back to when it happened and remembered she had been drinking a bottle of vodka at that time. She had become a secret drinker which helped her forget how sad she was feeling inside.

No one mentioned the alcohol and neither did she.

Walter had his suspicions about Helga's drinking but dismissed it and was just thankful she was OK. The house was mainly smoke damaged and the lounge room needed new furniture so Walter rallied his workmates together and in a few weeks everything was good as new. Helga realised how lucky she had been and how easily she could have died.

Chapter Twelve

After the fire Helga always smoked outside. She was drinking more openly now and she drank until she was drunk . Walter started drinking with her but not to the same extent. They started having parties on the weekends and had people over from their work places. Helga would flirt with Walters colleagues which made Walter feel embarrassed. Sometimes she would dance and flash her breasts at the guys. She enjoyed the men looking at her and liked to tease them.She told Walter she wanted men to want her and she was proving to herself that she was desirable to the opposite sex. Walter felt inadequate in the bedroom and Helga's flirting made him feel less of a man.

Walter decided that enough was enough and told Helga they were selling up and moving to Queensland.

He told her she needed to stop drinking as

she was embarrassing them both.

They sold the house and bought a new one in Springwood a suburb in south Brisbane. It was a large house with four bedrooms. Helga hoped their luck would change and one day those bedrooms would have their children in them.

Walter got a job as an electrician in a factory and Helga got a job as a receptionist at a doctors surgery. Things were fine and they settled in to the community well. They Made friends easily and were enjoying life.

One evening Walter answered a knock on front door. "Oh my good lord, come in , come in my dear friend " Walter said loudly. Helga jumped up and rushed forward to see who it was. "Helga, this is Yuri" he said.

Helga was impressed, he was as handsome as she remembered him all those years ago when they had first met. Very handsome

indeed. They talked for a few hours and discovered that Yuri was divorced and was living quite nearby . Yuri still liked to ride his bicycle and suggested that Walter should get a cycle and they could go cycling together sometimes. Helga watched Walter and Yuri talking and she could see the bond between them. It made her happy to see Walter so happy. Walter bought a bicycle the next day and before long he was out most weekends with Yuri.

Helga approached one of the doctors at the surgery and told him about wanting a family. She answered lots of questions about her menstrual cycle and also Walters health. The doctor sent her to see a doctor who was an Obstetrician who specialised in infertility issues.

Walter went with Helga to the appointment and they both had examinations. She was asked about the scars which covered her

body. She broke down as she told the doctor about the beatings and sexual abuse from her family and the doctor listened in horror.

The Obstetrician said he could find no internal damage. He suggested the reason Helga was not conceiving was a mental block. He made her an appointment to see a councillor. Walter had sperm tests and the results came back normal. His erection problem was a mental issue rather than a physical one and he was referred to a councillor too.

Helga was Angry. Blaming her in- capability to conceive on her past. She didn't even think about those times any more. She didn't go to the appointment. Walter went to see a councillor and he felt it was very helpful. Helga said it was bullshit and councillors knew nothing.

She started drinking again. Heavily.

Walter didn't notice her drinking as he hardly saw her those days due to the long hours he spent at work and his cycling trips.

One morning Helga announced to Walter that she was not going to work any more and was going to try and make clothing like her mother used to. She said she was not happy going to work as the women only talked about their children and she didn't want to hear that talk everyday. She said they were insensitive to her inability to conceive but Walter pointed out to her that no one knew that. Never the less Helga gave up her job.

Walter was ok with that as long as she was happy.

Helga was still secretly drinking.

Walter became interested in cars and started going to car shows with a few of his workmates. He loved fords and treated himself to a second-hand Ute. He taught himself how to service and do maintenance on it and cleaned it inside and out every other weekend. He still went cycling with Yuri and got him interested in old cars too. Their friendship was solid.

Helga wanted to learn how to drive so Walter instructed her although he wasn't keen on her driving his Ute. Many a swear word was said under Walters breath and his knuckles were white. He was so relieved that Helga passed the driving test the first time and she wanted her own car. Because Helga was not working they did not have enough money to buy another car but she persuaded him to get her one on a weekly payment plan. He thought if she had her independence she would stop obsessing about a baby. … and she wouldn't drive his ute.

Both seemed happy and life in Springwood was good.

One evening when Walter returned home from a car show with Yuri , there was a police wagon outside their home.

Walter ran into the house not knowing what to expect. Helga had been caught shop lifting. She was crying and apologetic and the policeman told Walter the shop did not wish to prosecute and Helga had been taken to the station for a verbal warning. Walter was shocked. When the police left he was enraged with her. "What the hell were you thinking you stupid woman" he bellowed at her. Helga flash-backed to her father shouting at her and waited for the beating that came next. Instead Walter stormed out slamming the door and she heard his Ute screech off down the street. Yuri was still in the passenger seat holding on for dear life. "Slow down. You'll kill us both " he shouted at Walter. When the Ute stopped in a parking bay Walter told Yuri what Helga had done.

Helga sat and thought about what she had done. She knew she had done wrong but she wanted those things so bad and couldn't afford them. She was remorseful and ashamed. She was a common thief.

When Walter returned home he had calmed down. Helga burst into tears and he held her in his arms and told her everything was going to be OK.

The next day Helga called Walter into one of the spare bedrooms and opened the wardrobe door. The wardrobe was stacked with clothes, shoes and accessories and as Helga pulled the items out Walter noticed baby blankets and clothing. He looked at Helga. He was speechless.

An appointment was made that day for Helga to seek professional advice from another councillor.

She continued to drink heavy and was nearly always a drunken mess when Walter came home from work. The house was a mess and never any dinner on the table. He ended up having to carry her up to bed most nights and put up with her shouting at him in undetectable slurs. He decided to sell the car and pay the loan off. He could not trust Helga behind the wheel drunk.

Walter had had enough. He loved Helga but she was driving him away. They never had a conversation any more and to see her in such a mess was heartbreaking for him. He decided to leave.

Helga tried to stop the drinking. She wanted Walter to come back. She went to her counselling appointment every week and she opened up and spoke of the sexual abuse she had experienced since she was

13. Talking about it brought it all to the front of her mind after she had suppressed it for so long. Every day she would think about her father and uncles mauling at her and the severe beatings she had from her father which had left her body and mind so scared.

The drinking blocked those memories and she would put the music on and dance around the lounge until she collapsed in a drunken mess on the couch. When she went out she would shout abuse at people and lift her top up and show of her breasts . She became the talk of the suburb.The local people started calling Helga the Danish lunatic because of the way she behaved.

The police were called out by the neighbours very regularly because of the loud music in the early hours and she used to throw empty bottles at the police and swear at them. She was also known as the drunk woman by the school kids who used to call her names when they went past her house. Walter was living with Yuri, going to work and continuing with his hobbies. Inside

he was worrying about Helga. He had heard she was behaving badly and he felt ashamed.He knew she was mentally unwell but others didn't and he was embarrassed. He prayed that she would get better.

Chapter Thirteen

Helga was committed into a mental hospital when she was 34 years old.

She had succumbed to putting long strands of cotton wool in her ears and rocking back and forth chanting quotes from the bible. The house was dirty and there were cockroaches everywhere. She stopped having conversations with anyone except with herself and ignored visitors like her old neighbours Alice and Raymond who travelled from Sydney just to see her.

Walter went to see her every Sunday in the institution but she stared straight through him.It was like he didn't exist. She was the love of his life and he prayed that one day with treatment she would return to the woman he had married.

Helga did not talk to anyone for over a year. She talked to herself and answered herself.

She did not speak to the staff but they reported that she was imagining she was having a conversation with someone she knew and was talking gibberish.

Walter moved back into the Springwood house. He paid off the home loan and made the house very inviting. He wanted Helga to come home and be comfortable and happy.

Eventually Helga started to improve and was put on some new medication that altered her mindset. She was calmer and she slowly started to communicate. She was not cured and she still chanted passages from the bible , swore a lot and lifted her top to show her breasts to strangers. Walter was told it would be challenging to take her home but decided she would be better off at home with him. In the car , driving into Springwood Helga let the window down and started shouting abuse at pedestrians. Walter cringed.

Over the next 6 months she had regular doctor visits and medication changes which improved her mood and she started to resume a reasonable lifestyle. She had to come to terms with the fact that she would never have a child and concentrate on building a good life for them both. She vowed another alcoholic beverage would never pass her lips again.

Walter was surprised at how quickly Helga got her life back on track. She never left the house and spent a lot of time sewing or knitting. She would ask Walter to hang out the washing and go to the shops as she didn't want to go outside.

They both knew that the neighbours talked about Helga being unstable and was a nut-case so they thought it best to move on.

They sold the house easily. It was a good property and Walter had added value by

doing renovations .They could afford a more expensive area and fell in love with a lovely property on mount Tambourine. It was a large house with a self contained annex on the side ,with views to the coast and the mountains..

Helga's thoughts were to rent out the annex to tourists in the summer months.

Their plan went ahead and the pair were happy. Walter gave up work and bought some cycles which they hired out to visitors. Yuri would visit often and he and Walter would cycle around the village and they would draw up cycling track recommendations for visitors . Walter maintained the cycles and kept them attractive with fresh paint and attached little baskets on the front. Helga made afternoon teas and scones. They had a good little business together.

Life on mount tambourine was slow and laid back. Helga still saw a doctor regularly and continued with her medications.

Helga was 36 years old. She felt older and wished she was younger. She felt reasonably well but sometimes she had horrible thoughts go through her mind about her past. She sometimes had nightmares or flashbacks to when her father was abusing her or her mother. She thought about uncle Rufus and uncle Robert having sex with her and felt guilty for enjoying it. She had always wanted someone to love her and she had the most wonderful man in the world loving her but she still felt empty.

Sex was seldom as Walter was always tired and he was having trouble maintaining an erection again. Helga said nothing as she didn't want to upset him. She started masturbating several times a week which gave her the pleasure but not the loving

contact that she yearned for.

She went to church every Sunday and she became friends with a younger man in his early twenties. His name was Trevor .

They started bible studies together for an hour after church each week and Helga got great comfort from religion.

One Sunday after church Trevor suggested they skipped bible study and go up to the mountain lookout point for a change of scenery. Helga agreed.

They started talking about their lives and Helga opened up to Trevor about her past.

She felt comfortable telling him of her abuse, drinking, mental issues and having to masturbate for pleasure. Trevor put his arm around her and kissed her passionately . From that kiss a sexual relationship was born and every Sunday after church 'bible study' became a secret sex session either in the open air or in Trevor s car. Helga went to church with no knickers on so it was easier for them to indulge. Sometimes he would put his hand up her skirt while they were in the church. Helga was loving this affair. Trevor knew how to please her. He had a large penis and he could last a long time.

She loved it when they had oral sex. Walter had never given that to her even though she had often pleasured him that way.

One Sunday when they were parked in a field Helga got naked and sat on the bonnet of the car with her legs spread open. Trevor got undressed too.

"Oh Helga, I want you so bad " he said. Hearing those words in that context turned Helga on. "Eat me first" she said as she grabbed his hair and pulled him down on her.

They were fully engaged in their passion and had no idea how long the policeman had been there ready to arrest them.

They were charged with an indecent act in a public place which meant a hefty fine and worst of all it was plastered on the front page of the Tambourine newspaper.

Walter was shattered. His heart was broken and he felt ashamed of his wife. Again.

Trevor left the area and Helga became withdrawn and stopped going out of the house.This was a patten she thought. Why was she always hurting Walter and herself.

Walter continued running the business and Helga helped, but their marriage was on the rocks.

Helga begged for forgiveness and Walter loved her so they sought help from a marriage guidance councillor.

The next year was spent working on their relationship and regaining the trust that had been lost.

The affair was never to be mentioned again.

Chapter Fourteen

Since Helga's infidelity The years had been kind to them both.Helga said it was the sunshine and fresh air that was doing them good. The business was doing very well and they had turned it into a little bed and breakfast. It was always booked out well in advance and Helga and Walter were very busy. Helga's mental health had been a roller coaster ride but she coped well. She saw a councillor every three months and was still on medication. But life was good.

It was 1976. Where had those years gone Helga asked herself. They had been in Australia for 21 years . She tried not to think further back than that. She knew it was a dark place.

She was 49 and they were planning a visit home to Denmark with a stop off in London to celebrate the Queen Elizabeth's silver jubilee and Helga's 50th birthday.

Helga was worried that going back to Denmark might be upsetting and was only really going for Walters sake.She never mentioned her uneasiness to Walter.

Christmas was their busiest time at mount Tambourine. The Annex and guest rooms were full and Helga and Walter had an old caravan on the property where they slept and rented out their own bedroom at these busy times.

When Walter had finished work at the house he went to the caravan where he found Helga crying with pains in her stomach.

"Walter , call an ambulance " she said. Seeing her face staring at him he ran back

up to the house and called the emergency service. Back down at the caravan he could hear Helga crying. She was in great pain. "What's wrong Helga?" He asked urgently. She let out a scream and dug her fingernails into his bare arms drawing a trickle of blood to the surface.

"I think I'm having a baby, Walter " she shouted at him between pants.

Walter froze. He was dumbfounded. "Walter" she screamed " I need to push"

Helga shouted instructions between contractions and Walter ran around panicking.

The ambulance turned up and the baby was delivered in the caravan. A baby girl.

Helga was taken to the hospital and had to stay two weeks because the baby was very small and Helga needed to be observed because of her age.

Their world had changed.

Helga hadn't know she was pregnant, her age had made her dismiss such a notion. She had noticed she had a larger stomach and her periods had stopped but put that down to the menopause. She was as shocked as Walter. As the fact sank in they were both ecstatic. They called their little miracle Crystal Greta after Walters mother and Helga's mother.

They hired in help so Helga could concentrate on caring for Crystal. Helga's dream had come true, she was at last a mother at 49 years old. Walter was so pleased and loved pushing the pram around the village. He felt proud and spoilt crystal at every opportunity . He had to keep looking at his daughter to check he wasn't dreaming. She was beautiful just like Helga, he thought.

Walter got a job at the brewery as a delivery driver whilst Helga continued to run the bed and breakfast with two employees to help out. Crystal was a good baby and Helga felt very lucky with the way her life was going.

They decided that they would keep the business going for 5 years and then move to the coast when Crystal was ready to go to school.

Helga embraced every day with love for Walter and Crystal. They were her blessing. She prayed to god to thank him for her happiness. She started attending church again every Sunday morning with her daughter. Walter did not attend. He didn't believe in god.

Helga met some new mother's at church and started going to morning teas during the week so she could talk and have support. She was older, a lot older than all the other women but had common ground with them through her child.

Crystal began crawling in no time and Helga was so excited. Walter was late home from his job at the brewery and She was eager to tell him about the first milestone. Walter was never late.

It was getting very late. Helga settled Crystal in her cot and started pacing up and down the room, looking out of the window for Walters car to come up the drive.

The phone woke her from her sleep. It took her a few seconds to get her bearings. She had dozed off whilst waiting for Walter. She answered the phone"Hello, Helga speaking " she said. She listened to the person on the other end of the line and then hung up.

She sat down in the armchair and it was so quiet she could hear the mantel clock ticking... getting louder and louder.

Helga started gently rocking back and forth chanting to god " please don't let him die, don’t let him die”.

Walter had suffered a heart attack whilst driving the delivery truck which had then rolled on the highway. He had been cut out of the cab and was in a critical condition at the Gold Coast hospital.

Helga was in shock. One of the employees heard Crystal crying when she arrived for work the next morning and went to investigate. She found Helga rocking in the chair.

The staff member fed and dressed Crystal and sent Helga to see Walter in a taxi.

Walter was in a bad way. He had a broken thigh and several broken ribs. A punctured lung and had suffered a stroke as well as the heart attack.He was paralysed down his left side and his speech was slurred . Helga was told Walter would survive but he would be hospitalised for a long time. Yuri offered to help.

Helga employed two more people to help keep the Bed and Breakfast running so she was able to visit Walter twice each week. Gradually Walter started to improve. He regained movement in his left side after several physiotherapy sessions and his speech was getting better. Helga was told she could take him home.

Walter had missed so many of Crystals firsts. She was crawling around so fast and could pull herself up to stand against furniture. She had two teeth and could say mum mum mum.

Walter looked at Crystal and there was such a likeness to his own mother there could be no doubt she wasn't his child. Deep down the thought had crossed his mind a few times when he was in hospital that Helga may have cheated on him again. But he could see she was his flesh and blood.

Walter started working at the Bed and Breakfast doing little jobs that weren't to strenuous and things began to improve for the little family. Helga looked at Walter and Crystal and counted her blessings.

Chapter Fifteen

In July 1982 Helga and Walter decided to sell their business and move to the Gold Coast.

Crystal was approaching her 6th birthday and would be ready to start school in a few months.

They put the B and B on the market and found a low set home in Miami Beach which they fell in love with. Crystal was excited because it had a pool.

A few days after the move they were on a plane to Copenhagen.

They hadn't gone back in 1977 as they had

planned because of the surprise birth of their beautiful daughter.They had obviously missed the Queen of England's jubilee but still stopped over in London to see the famous landmarks. They went to the Tower of London, London bridge, madam Tussaud's and Buckingham palace. Helga was hoping to get a glimpse of prince Charles and his new bride Lady Diana. But of course she didn't. They bought lots of souvenirs and postcards to remember the trip.

Arriving in Copenhagen gave Helga mixed feelings.The city remained as she had remembered it. The first stop was the hospital she had worked in many years ago.As she walked down the corridor to the maternity ward she felt a sense of excitement creep over her. The place was exactly as she had left it. The memories came flooding back and she smiled when she thought of those mother's emotions she had witnessed all those years ago.

Having given birth herself she now knew those feeling first hand. She smiled as she shed a tear of joy.

They stayed in Copenhagen a few nights and done some shopping. Helga wasn't sure if she wanted to go to Nuns Hospital where she had been treated badly. She left Walter with Crystal and took a bus on her own to the east side of the city. She entered the church where the nun had tapped her on the shoulder all those years ago and knelt at the alter. Helga prayed to the lord , thanking him for guiding her through her life and asked to be forgiven for her sins. When she left the church she knew she was forgiven.

She decided not to go to the nunnery.

Roskilde was still the quiet little town, Small and dull. The little shop where she worked was still there and Mrs Goldbergs name was still above the door. The bell tinkled as she opened the door and to her surprise she recognised Mrs Goldberg immediately. Helga stepped up to the counter and smiled " Hello Mrs Goldberg, do you know who I am?" She asked. The old lady studied her face and replied "oh my goodness, its Helga".

The shop was closed and Walter, Helga and Crystal were invited out the back of the shop for afternoon tea. It was a beautiful reunion and Helga told Mrs Goldberg about her life in Australia and the surprise arrival of Crystal.

Talk turned to Helga's family. She learnt her grandmother had died years ago and the three brothers, Ralph, Robert and Rufus had been living back in the old house in Roskilde . Helga shuddered.

The three men who had abused her all in Roskilde together!

Mrs Goldberg noticed the look on Helga's face and quickly added that her two uncles had left years ago but her father was now living upstairs in the pub and was very frail.she also learnt that Igor had remarried after their divorce and had seven children . Helga felt happy for him.

Back in Copenhagen Helga couldn't stop thinking about her father. Did she want to see him? Did she want to dig up the past? She had managed to suppress those memories for most of her life, should she risk the chance of bringing everything back to the surface?

Walter advised her against it. He said one flippant sentence which helped make her make up her mind. "Let sleeping dogs lie".

Instantly Helga was angered by the thought of her dog Billy, her beloved best friend who had been tortured and killed by her father. She need to tell her father what a nasty pig he was.

Walter took Crystal to the zoo while Helga

returned to Roskilde and to the pub to see her father.

Each step Helga climbed nearer to her fathers room she had flashbacks to climbing these stairs before and seeing her father naked with a prostitute. Her heart was thumping as she reached his door.

She knocked and waited. She knocked again the door opened and she looking straight into the face of a very old man. They looked at each other for seconds them seemed to Helga like an hour. "Helga? Is it you?" he said.

Helga went in and closed the door.

What was said inside that room didn't take long.

Chapter Sixteen

Back in Australia, in their new home on the Gold Coast life was glorious. Since returning from Denmark Helga seemed relaxed and happy.

Crystal started school and made lots of friends. She was very spoilt. Walter doted on her and gave her the best of everything. Helga got a part time job as a dental receptionist and Walter worked in a local garden centre.

Health wise Helga still visited a mental health councillor and Walter had regular heart specialist appointments but all in all they were doing OK.

Walter was still friends with their old neighbour from Springwood and they used to met up monthly and enjoyed going to old car shows and banger racing .Yuri had met a new lady friend who was taking up all his spare time so he wasn't around as often

any more .Helga got on with her sewing and hosting swimming parties for crystals school friends.

On crystals 10th birthday Walter got her a horse.They didn't have anywhere to keep it so they had to rent a paddock a few Kms away and take Crystal to see 'Magic' to ride her and feed and groom her everyday after school.

The novelty of owning a horse wore off pretty quick and Helga found herself having to tend to Magic. It was a burden Helga thought but continued to do the chore daily.

One afternoon when she was feeding Magic , Helga imagined Someone kiss her neck. She thought of Robert kissing her in the barn all those years ago and was physically sick. She shuddered and tried to push the thought from her mind but it kept coming to the surface. She didn't want to go groom Magic any more but she had to force herself. Her councillor said feeding the horse had triggered a memory from her past and she had to accept it had happened and move on because dwelling on it and analysing it in her head could set her back. Helga analysed it over and over in her head. Why had she liked it? Why had she wanted him to do it to her?

She came to the conclusion she was dirty and a sex addict. She kept that to herself.

One evening when Walter came home from a banger racing meeting Helga had made a lovely dinner for them both. Crystal was at a sleepover with a school friend so they had the place to themselves. Helga was sexily dressed and Walter got aroused as soon as he saw her. Dinner was missed.

Sex in every room was on the menu and at first it seemed possible. After round two Walter was exhausted and begged for a rest. Helga was still rearing to go. She fetched a large vibrator from the bedroom and used it in front of Walter. Walter was amazed he had never seen any woman self pleasure themselves before and he didn't know Helga had one of those things. He watched on getting aroused again.

They had more sex that night than ever before. They both liked it. Every time crystal went to a sleepover they had a wild night of sex.

It was Christmas and Helga decided to have a party. They invited workmates and old friends and neighbours .

They had children's games and gifts during

the afternoon and in the evening a friend took all the children to her house for another party and sleepover so the adults could party.

Helga hadn't had an alcoholic drink in years and had vowed never to drink again. Walter had a glass of wine and told Helga one wouldn't do any harm. So Helga had one. The party got rowdy and people in the street came and joined in. They played the music loud and danced in the garden. A couple stripped naked and jumped in the pool. Others followed.

The next morning the neighbours helped Helga and Walter clean up. Everyone had had a great time. Janet from up the street said the next party would be at her place.

Helga had only had the one drink and it had done her no harm. She was happy. Walter was happy.

Helga was about to go up to the paddock to

feed Magic when Derek from across the street called her over and handed her an invitation to a New Year's Eve party at his house. They chatted awhile and he invited himself to go with Helga to the paddock.

While feeding Magic Helga imagined being kissed on the neck. She continued chatting to Derek about the horse whilst trying to push those sexual thoughts from her mind. Derek had no idea that she was wanting him to rip her clothes of her and give it to her there and then. The feeling passed and they returned home.

New Year's Eve arrived and they party across the road was in full swing. Walter was already over there enjoying the fun but she was reluctant to go. She was not sure why but something was telling her not to go.

Helga fell asleep. A knock on the door awoke her. It was Derek. "Come on" he said Walter has sent me to get you.

Helga undone her blouse and exposed her braless breasts. "Come and get me" she said. Helga had given in to her sexual desire... again.

Magic was sold. Crystal had no interest and Helga didn't want the grooming duties any more.

Since New Year's Eve Helga had not ventured very far. Just to work and the shops. She had avoided Derek. She felt embarrassed and dirty.

Walters erection problem returned and Helga resorted to one of her vibrators for self pleasure.

Chapter Seventeen

When Crystal was 15 she got a part time job in a news agency. She was a very pretty girl and always respectfully dressed and polite. Helga and Walter were proud parents. She met a nice young boy who was also working at the news agency and they became inseparable. They were the same age and Alex came from a good family. Everyone was happy. Crystal had a dream of having her own restaurant and was doing business studies at school. Alex got an apprenticeship as a motor mechanic which pleased Walter. They got an old car and started tinkering with it at weekends. Walter and Alex got on very well.

When Crystal turned 16 Alex told Walter he wanted to marry her and asked if he could have her hand in marriage. Walter and Helga both thought she was too young. Walter told Alex to be patient and wait awhile. It was decided by Alex's parents

along with Walter and Helga that the couple could get engaged but were to both finish their studies before marriage.

Walter arrived home from work one afternoon and Derek was sitting in the kitchen. "Hello, Walt, I just called in to see how you and Helga were and to pass on an invite to Janet's party on Saturday night". Walter poured himself and Derek a glass of beer and went into the lounge room and left Helga to her chores.

Saturday night arrived and Janet s party

was buzzing.

Helga had a beer. Helga had a wine, Helga had another wine.

Helga had a dance with Derek and she could feel his hard penis pushing into her thigh. Walter was chatting to his wife molly, whom were both oblivious to the chemistry between their partners.

As the night went on people arrived and people left. It was another good party.

Someone suggested they had a partner swapping session. Everyone laughed at first and then some said yes. Helga looked at Walter and he winked and nodded to her. He was giving her permission to have sex with someone else. She had another glass of wine.

The next morning Helga had a hangover. She felt dreadful. Walter had a hangover too and they both sat quietly saying nothing. Helga was wondering if Walter remembered giving her the go ahead to have sex with someone else. She hadn't , but then she thought Walter may be thinking she had . Neither said anything. Helga thought it was time to stop going to parties.

Alex and Walter worked on the old car every weekend and decided to enter the next banger car race. Alex would drive.

Helga, Walter, Alex and Crystal started going to the old car racing every month and Alex had several wins under his belt. They had great fun.

One Saturday Crystal said she wasn't going to the banger racing as she felt unwell. Helga stayed home with her daughter and they cuddled up together and watched a film. Crystal asked her mother to tell her about life before she was born and Helga told her of a wonderful childhood with lots of friends and a lovely family. Helga made up a fantastic story which was completely opposite of the real life she had experienced. She didn't want her daughter to know of her past.

Crystal said she was so lucky to be born into such a beautiful family.

Alex finished his apprenticeship and asked again to marry Crystal. Although she hadn't finished her studies everyone agreed to the marriage and the wedding was arranged. It was a lavish wedding with lots of guests .The ceremony was on the beach and the reception was held in a hotel at surfers paradise. Walter paid for everything. Helga and Walter were very proud parents of the bride. Everyone was so happy.

The young couple got a rental house just around the corner from Helga and Walter and popped In to see them regularly. They still went car racing once a month and Alex would spend weekends with Walter, tinkering with old cars. Crystal finished her business studies and decided to do a chef apprenticeship. She started cooking meals for her parents and Alex's parents each weekend and she became very good.

On Crystals 18th birthday her parents gifted her $10,000 to help her start her own restaurant business. Helga helped her daughter by working in the kitchen 7 days a week.

Walter retired and his health was deteriorating. He was always tired and having dizzy spells. He did not mention this to Helga as he did not want to worry her. One morning Walter fell in the bathroom and couldn't get up or alert anyone. He eventually managed to crawl his way along the hall to the telephone and call an ambulance. Walter had suffered a stroke.Helga had to give up helping Crystal and stay home with Walter. The stroke had paralysed him on his left side like the stroke he had had before. Physiology was a great help and Walter gradually got movement back. It was a long process but he persevered and felt like his old self. Sadly Walter's sex drive had diminished. He could not get an erection let alone maintain one.

Helga masturbated regularly but missed the intimacy.

Crystal and Alex were running the

restaurant together and although they worked extremely hard the business was going downhill. Crystal told her parents she was closing down and would pay them back the $10,000.

Alex went back to a mechanic job and Crystal stayed home.

Helga visited her daughter regularly and when Crystal told her she was pregnant with twins she choked on her coffee. She was over the moon. She had never really thought of being a grandma. She went home to tell Walter the news. "Walter , Walter" she shouted as she opened the door. "You are going to be a granddad". Tears ran down his cheeks. He was so happy."Twins" she yelled, and Walter laughed and cried at the same time.

Walter knew Helga was masturbating and as much as he wanted to please her he just couldn't do anything.He couldn't even get into touching her.

One evening he asked Helga if she would have sex with another man if he gave his blessing. She said she missed the intimacy but wouldn't cheat ever again. Walter said it wouldn't be cheating and he understood she needed something he could not give.

Walter introduced Helga to an old friend from the banger racing club and then said he was going to a Physiology appointment. He left the house whilst his wife and friend were chatting. He was hurting but knew he was doing the right thing for Helga.

Helga liked Bob. They talked a lot and the conversation got to Walters problem and his request for Bob to give Helga what he couldn't.It was awkward and they both had a glass of wine to relax. After another glass of wine they kissed. That was the beginning of a long arrangement between the three of them. Bob visited Helga once a week and Walter would go out.

It was a good arrangement. Helga was happier. The sex was good.

The twins were born . Two healthy boys they named, Ryan and Wayne. The $10,000 Crystal had returned to her parents after the collapse of her business was given back to her to buy all she needed for the new family.

Grandma and granddad were so happy.

Chapter Eighteen

Helga's arrangement with Bob was still exciting. She loved their Friday afternoons. Bob was well endowed and always left Helga completely satisfied. He was good with his tongue too.

One afternoon they were having a session on the couch. Both completely naked preforming oral on each other.Walter walked in the front door and straight past them."Are you still here " he said.which was a statement more than a question.He slammed the kitchen door behind him and proceeded to make a cup of tea. The couple were at the point of no return and continued. Walter could hear his wife screaming with pleasure.He slammed the back door and went down to the garden shed. He put his head in his hands and cried.

Helga and Bob started having sex twice a week and sometimes they would go on a 'date' and have sex in his car.Walter said

nothing but inside he was jealous. Helga was unaware of Walters feelings as he had set up this arrangement and she thought he was happy that she was happy.

One evening Walter asked Helga if she was interested in travelling Australia now Crystal was settled with her own family.

Helga thought it was a great idea.

Walter talked to Crystal and offered her the

deeds to their house as a gift with the understanding that when they returned to Brisbane they would live in a granny flat that would be built on the property. Walter gave the deeds to crystal and a small one bedroom annex was built for when they returned.

Walter and Helga bought a camper van and planned a route for their trip. The boys were two years old when they set off. They were going to miss them terribly but would keep

in touch with phone calls, postcards and photographs.

Helga was going to do most of the driving as Walter still had a weak arm since his last stroke. They said their goodbyes and set off on their journey.

They headed up the Sunshine Coast and stopped at Harvey bay. It was beautiful. The camp site was modern with clean showers and a little camp shop. They met other campers who shared stories of their adventures and gave tips and advice and where and where not to go. They stayed there for the first 3 weeks. In the evenings they would meet with others and someone would pull out a guitar and start a sing along. Just like many films, Helga thought.

Helga was missing Bob. Missing sex. She had thrown away her vibrators before the trip so she used her hand. Walter's sex drive was zero.

Each week Helga sent a letter home to Crystal and sent a postcard and photos from each place they stayed. It was difficult for Crystal to send mail to her parents as they didn't stay in one place very long but they talked on the phone occasionally.Helga loved hearing about the boys and missed them so much.

Life on the road was fun. They saw some beautiful places and met some wonderful people. They slowly made their way up the Queensland coast. They did some fruit picking to earn some money to supplement their savings and enjoyed the outdoor lifestyle. Walter liked Cairns and they decided to stay a few months. He made friends with another camper who liked fishing and the pair spent lots of time on the water. Helga spent time at the camp site enjoying the sunshine and company of other campers.

Helga telephoned Crystal and told her the address of the campsite so she could send pictures of the twins.

Crystal sent lots of photographs of the twins. They were gorgeous boys and both looked like their mother. They weren't identical, but very much alike. Helga's heart melted. She closed her eyes and thought how lucky she was to have a beautiful daughter and two little grand sons.

Darwin was hot, very hot. It was Helga's 74th Birthday. Where had all those years gone she said to Walter as they sat in the restaurant. He reached across the table and held her hand. "I love you " he said.

They continued to send letters, postcards and photographs home.when Walter or Helga telephoned Crystal there was never an answer. They were disappointed but knew life was busy bringing up a family.

When they arrived in Broome they had been on the road for over a year. They were loving the freedom but both were concerned they hadn't heard from Crystal for quite sometime.

Sex was no longer an issue for Helga. Just laying beside Walter was enough. She smiled to herself when she looked back and thought she was over sexed back then and now she was too old.

Walter was slowing down considerably. He

was forgetful and losing interest in doing anything . Helga felt she was nagging him to even get up in the mornings.She asked him if he was feeling unwell but he said he was fine.

When they arrived in Perth they hadn't heard from Crystal in months..They were both worried.

Walter found the number of Alex's parents and rang them to see if they could shed any light on why they had not heard from Crystal. When Walter put the phone down he shuddered and sat quietly for a few minutes. Helga waited for him to tell her what he had learnt.

"We are going home" he said.

They were just about broke and Walter said they needed to get home fast. "Crystal has left Alex and the twins" he said. He also said he knew nothing more.

They sold the camper van which provided

them with enough money for air tickets to return to Brisbane.

Chapter Nineteen

Arriving at their old house and finding it had been sold was a shock. The new owners had just moved in and could not give a forwarding address for the previous owner.

They went to Alex's parents house where they found out that was where Alex and the twins were staying. No one knew where Crystal was.

Helga and Walter listened in disbelief as they heard that their daughter had got involved with a drug addict and left Alex for him.

She sold the house so Alex moved in with his parents. They learnt that Crystal was using drugs too.

With no savings left and only their pension they had to rely on Centrelink payments to rent a run down house in A run-down area of Brisbane . They had no furniture and had a second hand bed given to them by the local church. Alex's parents gave them a few items to help out.

Walter cried like a baby. To old to work, to old to provide for his wife. He was angry.

They tried to find Crystal but were unsuccessful.

"We gave that girl everything , even our home. Why would she leave those young children " Walter said to Helga. "What have

we become, we have nothing "

Helga cuddled up to Walter and cried herself to sleep.

She went to church every Sunday and prayed Crystal would come home. Walter sat in an old armchair that had seen better days. He was broken.

One weekend Alex visited with the Twins. He had heard Crystal was in the area with her boyfriend. But she had not contacted him. Walter wanted to go out looking for her but didn't know where to start. They had no transport either so they could do nothing. Helga's mental health suffered and she began rambling bible passages and rocking back and forth in her chair. She started smoking again despite Walters concerns . Alex popped in every weekend to bring her some rolling tobacco and papers. Walter enjoyed seeing the boys running around in the back yard . He was sad his daughter was not around to look after them.

Helga took to her bed and wouldn't get up.she went to the toilet and that was it. She stayed in her bedroom listening to a religious channel on the radio and sang hymns.Walter slept on a single bed with broken springs in another bedroom. He provided her with simple meals and endless cups of coffee. She would not engage in conversation with him. It was Christmas time and very hot. They had no air

conditioning, Only a small desk fan and it was extremely hot and humid.On one of Alex's visits Helga was in bed wearing a winter coat, scarf and fur hat. Alex said she needed to see a doctor as she had lost her mind and she hadn't had a wash in weeks. Alex called a doctor to visit Helga. Walter protested when the doctor called an ambulance to take her to the local hospital for a mental assessment. She was committed to a mental institution out west.

Alex took Walter to see her once a fortnight but she was a mess. She swore at Walter sometimes and she had no idea who he was. Other times she would be quite alert and asked about Crystal and the twins. Alex said it was probably something to do with the time she had her medication.

Walter watched TV all day every day. He even slept in the broken armchair as it was more comfortable than the bed. Alex

brought him groceries every week.

One afternoon there was a knock on the front door. Walter was startled as no one ever came to the door except Alex, and he had a key. Walter shouted " Who is it, what do you want?" There was no answer and another knock. He muttered and puttered as he got up and shuffled to the door. His body was stiff from sitting so long in the same position. As he stared at the woman standing in front of him she said "Hello Dad". Walter gripped the door handle to steady himself . "Crystal" he whispered .

Crystal fell into her dads arms and they hugged for awhile, neither saying anything. Walter was silently crying inside. His daughter had come home.

As Walter opened his eyes and looked over Crystal's shoulder he noticed a scruffy looking fella standing near the gate. "That's Jimmy , my friend"

Walter spent the next few hours listening to his daughter's story about how she had become addicted to drugs. What happened to the money she got from selling the house. What were her plans.

Walter learnt his daughter had met a guy at a party who introduced her to cannabis. He told her she was beautiful and he was in love with her. She bought weed from him secretly, got into a passionate affair and became addicted to him and the drugs. Her addiction had escalated quickly and she started snorting cocaine. It was expensive and she was in debt. She had sold the house to pay her debts and left Alex and the twins to go with Brad to WA.

She had been living wild. Paying for herself and Brads lifestyle and when she ran out of money he had left her. She told Walter she had needed coke and had been selling herself for drug money.

She had met Jimmy who brought her back to Brisbane. She was still a drug addict.

Walter allowed Crystal and Jimmy to stay that night in Helga's bed. He sat in his armchair all night wide awake trying to process what he had learnt.

The next morning he told his daughter she could stay for awhile so she could try and get her life back on the right track.

Crystal wanted to visit her mother but Walter said he needed to break the news to Helga first as the shock of seeing her daughter might affect her mentally and he wanted the doctors advice.

The news Crystal was Home was wonderful news for Helga.

Crystal went to visit her with her father and the three of them cried together .

When Walter and Crystal got back to the house Jimmy had gone and so had Walters watch and the few dollars he had in the bedside cabinet. "Bastard" they both said together.

Chapter Twenty

Crystal stayed with Walter. She saw the twins weekly but not Alex. He had met another lady and didn't wish to see Crystal.

She was happy with that.

She was still using drugs. Walter didn't know where she got the money from and didn't ask. She was going out every night and sometimes not coming home all night. Others times she brought a stranger home to bed.

Walter didn't like these strangers in his home but he didn't say anything to Crystal about it because he was frightened she may leave. Helga was improving and he didn't want anything to knock her back.

It was Walters 75th birthday and Helga was coming home for the weekend. Crystal baked a cake .

Helga had a good afternoon. Alex's parents

dropped the twins off to spend sometime with their mother and the other grandparents. The boys were laughing and running around the house and garden. Helga felt happy.That evening Crystal was sitting out on the front veranda smoking a joint. Helga went outside and sat with her daughter. "Give me a drag" she said. "Mum"said Crystal. "Go on please, I want to try it" Helga replied. Crystal passed the joint to her mum.

She coughed a little and then took a second draw. " it doesn't do anything" she giggled.

Before long Helga was finding everything funny and laughing loudly. Walter went to see what was so funny and he was angry to see his wife smoking a joint"Helga, you are 75 years old, what are you doing" he yelled."Sharing a joint with my daughter, you old fuddy duddy " she replied and roared with laughter.

After that weekend Helga's health improved dramatically. The doctors said she could be released from the institution if Walter could manage her at home.

Walter moved back into the bedroom with Helga and a second hand double bed was given to them by a neighbour for Crystal.

They didn't have much but they were grateful they had a roof over their head and food. Crystal always bought Helga tobacco. She was still smoking weed and going out all night. Walter told Helga that he thought their daughter was getting money for the drugs through prostitution.

They weren't happy about that but they couldn't risk losing her.

One morning when Walter got up there were to guys in the lounge smoking weed. He was angry and told them to get outside. Crystal came from the bedroom with

another guy and asked them all to go outside.

Walter was really angry. Why were there three strangers in his home he asked her.

Crystal sat down and cried. She told Walter

she had met them in a bar the night before and she had brought them back for paid sex so she could pay her dealer before he broke her legs. Walter laughed and said she had been watching too much rubbish on TV.

Crystal was sobbing and said it was true, she owed over $3000.

Walter looked into her eyes and believed her. He had no money or nothing to sell. He had no way of helping her raise the money.

He told her to let the men back in and he went back to his bed with Helga and turned the radio volume up.

Men continued to come and go. Crystal

spent most days in bed and Walter and Helga watched TV, Sitting in their broken armchairs. What had their lives become.

Helga and Walter wanted their daughter off the drugs and asked Alex for advice.They asked a councillor to come to the house and talk to them as a family.

It was an interesting session and they had options of help available as long as Crystal wanted to quit. She said she did.

Walter was in the back yard when he heard Helga yelling. Inside he found her standing at the kitchen sink , crying.

Helga had gone into Crystals room and found her with a tie being used as a tourniquet and a needle in her arm. Crystal was shooting up. Walter was furious.

He burst into Crystal's room and told her to pack her bags and leave. Crystal was high,

she swore abuse at them both and slammed the front door as she left. Surprisingly Helga was calm. She thought of when she was young,the incest, her sexual antics. Who was she to judge. Her daughter was an adult and she was making her own choices. Walter said she would probably come back when she had nowhere else to go,

Crystal had been gone a few weeks and Helga and Walter spent their days watching TV. They didn't talk much. Helga seemed fine to Walter , despite the fact she was doing some odd things.They went grocery shopping in a taxi on pension days and Helga started getting a can of cat food every week. She opened the can when she got home and put it behind the TV cabinet. She said it was to feed the rats. Walter let her get on with it, he was too tired to argue.

Walter had been right. Crystal turned up one evening begging forgiveness. She wanted to get clean with her parents help.

Crystal went to rehab by her own free will. It was going to be hard but she was positive. Helga was positive too. Walter wasn't so sure.

One night the old couple sat in their armchairs watching TV when a clutter came from behind the TV cabinet and then a big brown rat came scurrying out across the lounge floor. Walter screamed and Lifted his feet up high. Helga sat still and the rat sat on her feet. "Oh. he is so soft and warm" she said.

Helga tamed that rat. She named him Hugo. In the evenings Hugo would sit on Helga's lap and be fed scraps from her dinner plate while they watched TV. Walter thought his wife was cuckoo but he loved her still the way he always had.

Crystal completed the rehab and came home. She kept apologising for what she

had done. She was very remorseful about leaving the twins, selling the house and letting her parents down.She got a job as a waitress in a hotel restaurant.

Walter missed driving. He missed tinkering with cars. He started putting a few dollars away each week to buy a cheap car he could work on. Helga spent lots of time in bed with Hugo sleeping on her chest. Crystal and Walter both noticed Helga was not quite mentally healthy but she seemed happy so they didn't seek her any help.

Walter was sleeping on his broken armchair again and Helga had the double bed. Walter didn't even go into the bedroom any more as it didn't smell very nice and there was cat food on the dressing table and on a saucer on the floor.

Crystal could hear noises coming from the ceiling and suspected more rats. She called in the rodent control. Helga sat watching TV when the pest inspector turned up. She talked to the man through the fly screen, denied any rodent problem and told him to bugger off. Crystal and Walter tried to explain to her that rats carried diseases and weren't good for her health but she wouldn't listen. "They are god's creation,I love all god's animals " she told them.

Walter bought an old Car with his savings and enjoyed sitting in it listening to the radio. It needed a lot of work to get it roadworthy but he was happy just sitting behind the wheel and imagining he was on a road trip.

It was a hot day and Helga had woken early. She looked up at the ceiling and made pictures with the shadows like she used to do when she was a young girl. She thought back to her childhood bedroom, her dog Billy and her father. She pushed those thoughts out of her mind and got up. Walter was already sitting in his car on the front drive. Helga made a pot of tea and called Walter in. They were sitting in their armchairs drinking tea when Crystal came through from the bedrooms. She emptied the washing machine and went to hang the wet clothes on the washing line. Walter washed their cups and went back to his car and Helga watched TV with Hugo on her lap.

The scream was piercing . Walter heard it above the music from the radio. "Walter, Walter, Walter" he heard Helga yelling, "Help,Help, please Help" Walter went towards Helga's voice. She was screaming hysterically. As he neared the shed he saw Crystal hanging from the rafters with a noose around her neck. Helga had her arms around Crystals legs as if trying to push her upwards to take the weight of her neck. Walter stood looking at them. The shock had froze him to the spot. A neighbour pushed past him and helped Helga lift Crystal to ease the pressure of the rope. Walter hurried forward and cut the rope with a pair of garden shears. They heard the ambulance siren in their street . The neighbour said he could feel a pulse. Helga and Walter hugged each other as Crystal was put onto a stretcher .

Chapter Twenty-one

Three people were at the cemetery as Crystal was lowered into the grave. Helga , Walter and Alex. The family felt the twins were too young to attend their mother's funeral.Walter and Alex held Helga as she sobbed uncontrollably at the loss of her daughter.

After the funeral Helga took to her bed . She unfolded the crumpled piece of paper she had been clutching in her hand and started to read.

All it said was 'sorry mum'.

Helga sobbed.

The house became a shrine. Crystals photographs were placed everywhere with cheap plastic religious icons beside them. There were candles on the windowsills, but they weren't lit.

Walter sat in his broken armchair next to Helga sitting in hers. Hugo the rat sat on her lap. They didn't eat for a few days and they hardly spoke.

Chapter Twenty-two

One Saturday a few months after Crystals death, Alex visited with the twins. He was shocked at the state of the house. It was filthy and he could smell an unrecognisable stench.He tidied up a bit and made them a drink. There was only mouldy food in the cupboard so he went to the shop and bought some essentials. He thought he would have to do something about how they were living as this was not right. Helga was behaving strange and talking about god wanting her to save all the little creatures. Before Alex left he had a quick look around the house.He jumped back in disbelief as he entered Helga's bedroom and saw thousands of cockroaches scurrying over her bed.

"Helga, why are all those cockroaches in your room?. That's disgusting" he yelled.

She told him to leave her little friends alone. She had lost the plot, Alex thought.

The authorities turned up at the house with pest control and Helga would not let them in. She waved her walking stick at the men and told them there was no rats or cockroaches in the house. Walter stood behind her and backed her up "Bugger off" he yelled.

They didn't return.

For the next year Helga and Walter became reclusive. Although Alex had remarried he still felt an obligation to keep an eye on his ex in laws. Every week he went to the shops and got their groceries and Helga's cigarettes.Helga would shout out to him " Alex, you sexy man, come get in my bed". He left the the groceries just inside the front door and hurried away . The smell which came from inside made him feel sick. He dare not imagine what the smell was.

Helga was staying in her bed for days. She wore her old winter coat and a fur hat. Walter sat and slept in the old armchair and had the TV on 24 hours a day.

He made coffee for them both and Helga

demanded instant mashed potatoes several times a week.

The rats had multiplied and the neighbours complained to council that they had been seen going into Helga's house. The authorities called again with pest control and this time Walter let them in. Thousands of rodent carcasses where found in the roof space. The men were recovering sacks full. She protested and cried as Hugo was taken from her.

Helga was taken to the mental heath ward at the hospital for assessment and Walter went to the general ward to be assessed for health issues related to their recent living conditions.

Walter had a few infectious bites on his body and was kept in for treatment and observation. Helga was admitted to the mental institution, again. She never had a single bite mark on her body.

While they were both in hospital environmental services went into their home. There was rat droppings everywhere. Thousands of dead and alive cockroaches were in Helga's bedroom. Cockroaches were crawling out of a hole that Helga had made beside her bed. It was discovered that she had been putting mashed potato in the hole to feed the little creatures.

Behind the TV was a massive hole where the rats had been getting in and piles of dried up cat food which Helga had been put there to entice them.

The house was repaired , cleaned and fumigated.

The owner of the house wanted to help Helga and Walter and bought some second hand furniture from the Salvation Army.

Walter went back to the house. Alex

arranged for someone to go in once a day to check on him and make sure he was OK .

He sat in his chair day and night with the TV on 24 hours a day.

The chair was clean and comfortable.

Helga remained in the mental hospital. She recited the bible and sang dirty ditties.The staff enjoyed looking after her because she was funny.

Walter missed Helga. He hadn't seen her for months. He told Marie, the lady who was coming in everyday he wanted to see his lovely wife Helga.

Marie wasn't supposed to get involved in her clients personal affairs but she was human and wanted to help Walter. She decided to take him to visit Helga.

Marie was so glad she had taken Walter and to see both their faces light up when they saw each other would stay with her forever. The old couple held each other tightly and they both shed a tear.

Helga slowly started to improve and she was allowed to go home as long as Marie went in twice a day to give medication and help with meal preparation. Walter and Helga were both happy with that and they looked forward to seeing Marie everyday. The house was clean and tidy and they were eating well.

One morning Walter said to Marie, "is this woman sitting next to me my wife?"   Marie replied "yes , it's Helga"

Walter looked at Helga and said "I thought I married your sister"

Helga was angry. She grabbed her walking stick and hit Walter on the shins very hard.

Marie noticed changes in Walter. He

thought he was in the wrong house and

wanted to be taken home. One morning he said he had heard the soldiers coming during the night and he had hidden in the wardrobe.

Marie reported the changes and he was diagnosed with vascular dementia. He needed more care than Marie could provide and although she wasn't supposed to, she gave them her telephone number in case they needed help at anytime.

Helga started taunting Walter. She told him he had always been useless in the bedroom and she had liked having sex with other men who knew how to please her. She told Marie about Felix on the ship and her sexual encounters with Derek while Walter sat listening. Marie felt embarrassed. Walter told Helga to shut up and her sister was better looking than she ever was. He said he didn't believe he had married her and she was a lair. Marie felt bad for the pair of them but sometimes she had to smile at what was said.

Marie's phone rang around ten o'clock one night and it was Helga. Walter had fallen in the bathroom and she couldn't get him up. Marie rushed over to their house to find Walter laying on the floor, naked, covered in his own faeces. He had diarrhoea , missed the toilet and slid over. The smell made Marie vomit. A few minutes later an ambulance arrived and the men wrapped him in a blanket and got him onto a stretcher. They took him to hospital for a check up.

Helga got the mop and bucket and started to clean up the bathroom. She started to giggle. She said to Marie " silly bastard slipped on his shit" she gave a great big belly laugh until she cried . She sat down and Marie carried on cleaning the bathroom.

Walter came home the following morning and he was very confused.He walked along the hall looking for the stairs to go up to his bedroom. He argued with Helga and Marie that there were stairs to go to his bedroom but he couldn't find them.

Helga called him a stupid man.

Chapter Twenty Three

Marie arrived at the house at her usual time on a Monday morning to find the door opened and no one at home. She called her boss and he told her to go home and call back later. Marie was just about to leave when she saw Helga coming up the street waving her walking stick.

"Walter has gone, my Walter has gone" she was yelling. Marie learnt that Walter thought he was in the wrong house and thought he still lived in Mt Tambourine and left to go home to his own house. Helga had tried to follow him but she was to slow. Marie called her boss again and he said he would report him missing.

Walter had been missing for 36 hours.The police helicopter was searching the area and the neighbours were looking in their back yards. There was no sign of him.

Helga prayed to the lord he was safe and

she chanted forgiveness for her sins.

Three weeks went by and although the police were still looking Helga had made up her mind he was dead. She stayed in her bed with her coat and fur hat on and refused to eat. Marie sat with her in her room everyday and listened to Helga reciting bible verses.

Then the news came that Walter had been found. He was alive but very frail. He had only been a few streets away. A woman had found him sitting by her front gate and had helped him up and into her house. Walter did not know his address . So she had let him stay awhile. He hadn't been eating much and was still wearing the same clothes. The woman had a visitor and he recognised Walter from a poster.

When Helga heard the news she got out of her bed. She started to eat and had a shower. Marie was pleased Walter had been found and Helga's mood had changed. She was happy.

The next day Marie took Helga to see Walter in the hospital .

Walter said "Hello Helga, where is Anna?"

Helga was hurt that he had asked after her sister. She told him he was a nasty old man and left.

Sadly Walter had a massive heart attack at the hospital that night and passed away.

Helga was distraught. Distraught that her husband had passed on and regretful she had called him a nasty old man . She continued to live at the house on her own and Marie still went in everyday.She sat in her old armchair and watched TV , rolling her own cigarettes and smoking one after the other. Little burn holes peppered her clothing and she thought it was funny to burst in to the chorus of the old Hymn ,Holy, Holy ,Holy. Several times a day.

Helga told Marie her life story, about the abuse and incest, her desperation and obsession of wanting a child. Her infidelity and mental breakdowns. She told Marie all she wanted was to be loved.Marie shed a tear that night. Poor, poor Helga, she thought.

Eventually ,Helga went into an aged care facility as she needed constant care.Marie kept in touch by visiting occasionally.

She talked to the staff about her life but she knew no one was actually listening. They didn't have the time.

Helga laid on her bed and looked up at the ceiling. She made memories with the shadows. She saw her father and uncles looking at her on her left , Anna and Crystal on her right. In the middle she saw her dog

Billy and Hugo the rat. She closed her eyes, smiled and whispered Amen.

As she drifted off to sleep she saw Walter waving in the distance.

Printed in Great Britain
by Amazon

77490170R00117